Violet's Secret

Violet's Secret

LORI RILL

Text design by: Vince Pannullo
Print by: RJ Communication.

Printed in the United States of America

ISBN: 978-0-9850100-0-3

For my devoted husband
without your confidence and love,
this book would never have begun or ended.

"Be yourself. Everyone else is already taken."

— Oscar Wilde

Chapter 1

I T'S not as if everyone accepts everyone else for who they are, but there aren't as many secrets since Winter Solstice last December. I still keep a lot about myself underneath my cloak, so to speak.

"Here, taste this," Mom said, as she held out a frosted cupcake that had a bite removed from the side facing me. The soggy pleated paper was already peeled away from the yellow cake, brown on the edges.

I wrinkled my nose, but I took it from her, unpeeled more of the paper and nibbled a small bite. "Mmmm," I said, nodding my head in approval. "The frosting is a funny color though. It looks like, uh," I hesitated, not wanting to hurt her feelings.

"Seaweed. Yeah, I know," Mom tilted her head looking at the top of the cupcake, and then she gestured at me to finish it. "I was trying to mix some food coloring, and instead of a pretty purple, it turned like a greenish brown. I'll figure it out." She turned back to her mixing bowls and measuring spoons laid along the length of the counter in the kitchen.

"Well, it tastes good," I said, breaking the cake off into bite-sized pieces and trying to neatly put them in my mouth without crumbs falling off. "D'you want some help?"

"Of course," Mom answered.

My mother makes a grand cupcake. My mother didn't make much that we could brag about, but she put her heart into it all.

On my thirteenth birthday, she made trays of cupcakes especially for me. It was my Bat Mitzvah, a special coming-of-age ceremony followed by a party, a part of the Jewish traditions that my family celebrates.

I was the centerpiece of my party. I don't ever like the spotlight, but on that day, it was all about me. I smiled a whole lot. I wore a sparkly purple dress. It hit just nicely above my knees so that I could show off lacy tights in a lighter shade of purple. Mom said it had timeless elegance; it had sleeves that hugged my elbows like wrinkly socks would cuddle my ankles, as comfortable as slippers. The dress felt perfect. Mom also said that the square neckline needed something, and she knew just what that was.

That's when she gave me my violet necklace. It was something so simple, yet so personal. Its color and beauty matched me so naturally. I can't explain it. I remember doing my hair in my bathroom in front of the mirror, fanning the door back and forth to rid the room of the steam from the shower. My dress and tights were lying on my bed, ready for me to give them life, and Mom came in with no words, just a really big grin, so big it seemed suspicious, like she was up to something devious. Instead I think it was that she could barely hold in surprises. She didn't have much to give in terms of things, gifts and such that cost money, but she gave so much of her spirit. Her time was what she usually gave me, and I was satisfied with that. But that day, counting down to my real birthday, she gave me my violet. And I'm sure that day it was like an angel got its wings. I swear I heard bells ringing in my ears. It wasn't exactly bells.

I'm beginning to understand more and more about my unusual ability, what I can see, what I can hear. It always seemed normal to me to see all the colors. I don't remember how young I was, but I was probably five or six when Dad said that people call the colors "auras" and that I should try not to tell everyone all the time what I could see. I didn't know how to explain it anyway, so I just got used to reading people's moods and personalities and didn't say much about it to them.

I remember there was this lady who worked in the grocery store who was always so nice, and it seemed like the sun shone around her round face. I used to think that everyone saw her that way, but when Dad and I would go shopping, he laughed when I called her the sunny lady.

"What are you talking about, Violet?" he asked, shaking his head. "Who's the sunny lady?"

I started to point to her behind the customer service counter, and Dad pushed my arm down and whispered that pointing wasn't polite. Staring right at her, I whispered back, "The lady with the sun around her face. She likes being nice to everyone all the time. She tries really hard to be that way."

Dad looked at me with a confused look that quickly disappeared, and he never questioned my assessment of the sunny lady. We just accepted it and secretly agreed not to talk about it.

It became harder not to tell my friends though as I grew a little older, just because it seemed so natural. I never thought that anyone would think it was weird or frightening. In the elementary school music room, a place I always liked to go because Mom had been teaching me how to play the piano, I would distribute the instruments to my classmates on days we'd get to play. The other kids would ask me how I knew which instrument they really wanted that day. I would just shrug my shoulders, smile, and continue putting a set of cymbals on one desk, a metal triangle on the next, and so on. On days that we'd sing instead of play, the teacher would catch me humming the tune of the song we were about to learn as I walked by her on my way into the classroom. She'd give me a shiny sticker and urge me on to my seat. It was fun to be good at something, something special, and eventually just expected from me, I guess.

It was this new girl who made me feel like keeping it all a secret. I didn't like her from the start, but I wasn't brought up in a manner that would let me show it, so I just avoided her. It was third grade, and we were doing multiplication tables on worksheets, as many as we could in a minute's time. Our teacher was settling the girl into a desk next to mine, and I could see her colors. Like a rotting apple, soggy brown with spots of red that hadn't given up to the decay.

"What are you staring at?"

These were her first words to me. I forced myself not to look and listen to her, but I had difficulty keeping her colors and thoughts away from my own. She didn't like me, and I could tell. I think I frightened her, but I didn't understand that then. I stopped handing out instruments in music class and telling my friends what was for lunch when I knew they were hungry or even answering questions in class right before the teacher asked them. I think everyone has a time in her life when she feels judged. That was my first.

Wearing the necklace the day of my Bat Mitzvah gave me confidence, made me feel like I could do anything. It made that day feel like a holiday. I was celebrating and not worried about what anyone was thinking about me. I knew now that I could decide whether I wanted to listen. Not to what they were saying to me, but what they were thinking. At first I wasn't sure it was right to listen to their thoughts. With my violet, Mom assured me that today was my day, so I didn't know what else to do except to listen.

I knew how nervous Dad was for me before my Bat Mitzvah. I had to read and chant prayers and portions of the Torah in front of everyone, and even though I'd practiced (a lot more than I would've liked), I had those funny flips going on in my stomach.

Dad wasn't drinking as much coffee as he normally did before we left the house; he said his stomach was upset, but I remembered feeling like he had told me that he was nervous for me, but he had confidence in me. He knew I was smart and prepared for my big day and that we'd all remember this for a lifetime. Later on, I wasn't sure I had ever really heard him utter the words.

Sometime during the ceremony, while I was at the podium and all my friends and the small family we had was gathered on the graham cracker-colored benches cushioned with banana-colored velvet, I concentrated on finishing my parts, reading and singing and chanting. But after a while, I couldn't ignore all the noise. I glanced up from the words I was reading to the expansive room that needed voices and music to fill it up; it overwhelmed me, making me feel small and dormant. The sanctuary opened so tall before me with its two-story stained glass windows and its towers of wood encasing the stage and corners of the seats. A little wrinkle formed on my forehead between my brows as I noticed that no one else seemed distracted by the noise while I continued my prayers. It wasn't like a deafening concert that made my ears numb or a room full of echoes and water showers, like when I'm close to a fountain or inside the atrium of the mall. It was a rush of words that I couldn't decipher; it ebbed and flowed like waves of water. It didn't scare me. It intrigued me, especially when I began to pick out the conversations.

Mindy, my best friend, was sitting with her family. I saw her there, and it gave me confidence, made me smile. I always understood Mindy well; it was like I didn't have to ask what she was thinking. I just kind of knew. Today, it felt that way with a lot of people in the room. I know I must've looked like I was daydreaming. But I was just trying to figure it all out. I was just glad I didn't stop reading, and I continued with the Rabbi's directions and leadership.

Guests and family who came up to me during the party said

how beautiful the service was. They always say that. I mean, what else are they going to say? But I was glad. Especially for Mom and Dad. They wanted it to all work out perfectly. I was their only shot at it, of course. No other kids for them to mess up with, so I pretty much had to do it right the first time. They really were easy-going, and I smiled proudly that I lived up to their expectations.

She really sounded beautiful.
It was a beautiful service.
She looked lovely in purple.
That's her favorite color, you know.

I lay my freshly painted fingernails across the violet necklace and became familiar with its feel under my fingers and around my neck. I saw the colors, and my parents were encouraging me to read them and really listen.

As we left the temple, Dad put his arm around my shoulders and held Mom's hand on his other side. It had been a long day, one of those that I was only realizing how tired I was now that it was over. We had a luncheon after the service, when we were able to talk with all of our guests. I must've said "thank you" a thousand times. We strolled slowly through the parking lot to our car.

"We are so proud of you. You worked hard and it showed today." Mom sighed. "My Little Violet," she said affectionately. She was conflicted about my growing up and wanting me to remain her baby girl.

I always tell Mom everything. She said that she was glad that I did because some day, when I was a torrid, unbearable teenager (her words, not mine), that I'd probably trade in talking to Mom for talking to my friends. It was hard for me to imagine not ever wanting to tell Mom everything. In fact, I told Mom about listening to all I had heard that day during my Bat Mitzvah and how I felt more in control of reading the colors than ever before. I felt energy, and maybe the violet around my neck nurtured it. I ignored the change I saw in Mom's eyes. I sometimes wished that I hadn't told her so much that day. Because a few months after the party, when the holidays came around and it was a time when most people would start feeling the holiday spirit, Mom was gone.

My mother was not my best friend. My mother was my mom—she put her arm around me and held me close to her side, protecting me from the large, loud, black lab who barked when I wanted to play hide 'n seek in our backyard. She taught me how to put on pretty purple dresses and brush my hair off my face so that my murky gray-blue eyes stood out. She read books with me at night even when I knew she was tired and just wanted to snuggle under the covers and close her own eyes for the night. I miss her.

I still carry her memories with me in my dreams. She has not been by my side since last September, and it is now December, a year later. She has left me wondering how I am going to learn how to become a woman and a mother myself someday without her guiding words and affectionate hugs and kisses.

I have her violet charm around my neck, which makes me feel stronger than I've ever felt in my life, even when Mom was in my life. The stem of the violet is wrapped on a slim black cord. The charm is a couple inches in length and has tiny jade leaves that fold in on themselves and help the stem grasp the cord. The violet itself sometimes rolls over on my chest as if it is hiding, but I like to turn it so that its shimmery violet petals draw in the light of lives around me. Sometimes the smooth teardrop petals sparkle with lavender splashes; while other times, they darken and have depth to them, almost like black pools that seep into my chest. I can actually feel the heaviness when the violet changes color like that. It weighs on my heart more than anything else and gives me an uncertain feeling about what's going on around me, even though I can't seem to see that anything has changed in front of my eyes.

It's been tough, but Dad and I have been making it through together. After my Bat Mitzvah, all the energy I had been feeling wore me out to the point that I was starting to feel so weak that I couldn't get out of bed. Listening to everyone around me must have been too much, I thought. I just couldn't think clearly; school felt jumbled and chaotic, and for the first time ever, my grades were going down. But the end of seventh grade for me was on the field hockey field. I played on the team with Mindy, mostly because she wanted to, not because I was good at it. It had been a long game, and I collapsed at the very end. That was when I went to the hospital and spent most days sleeping off what the doctors figured was exhaustion. I have fuzzy flickers of my dad visiting me, bringing me books to read if I felt up to it and some of my favorite snacks which I ate in small doses.

When I finally seemed to have more and more days that I spent awake instead of asleep, they sent me home. But my mother hadn't waited out my hospital stay. She was gone. Mom wasn't the strongest of personalities, and I've heard that illness or tragedy can be the cause of marriage trouble. I know plenty of people at school whose parents break up or divorce, but I never thought that I'd be one of those people. My last thoughts were that I had hurt her, but although he seemed more hurt and lost than I, Dad reassured me that it wasn't anything I had done. We were going to have to rely on each other from now on.

"Sometimes people grow apart," he said.

I could see something different behind those words. But I couldn't seem to clean off the lie from the truth. I would continue to struggle with Mom's leaving us, because I knew she loved us. I just didn't know what to do. So, although I didn't completely buy his explanation, it would have to suffice because he wasn't much of a talker in the first place, and I wasn't able to get through to any thoughts different from what he told me.

I tried my hardest that whole summer to listen to Dad's thoughts. I wasn't sure sometimes whether I wanted to hear what I might hear. I could easily see his colors, mostly waterfalls of blue. I knew how the sad tears inside him felt because I missed her too, but if there was something hidden there, I couldn't find it. I treasured my violet necklace even more than ever as we tried to get back some sort of normalcy.

Walking into the cafeteria from my eighth grade English class, I felt compelled to hold the violet with the tips of my fingers and bring it up to my lips. I didn't kiss it; I just held it in front of my mouth and took a small, deep breath. As I exhaled, I sensed that my violet was turning a shade of purple, like plums, the ones we buy at the grocery store that look like little footballs and have just a few bites of summer juiciness inside. I dropped my pendant out of my fingers and let it fall with a bounce onto my skin, and I placed my palm over it for a brief second, thinking about my mom. My stomach jolted as if I've just gulped down a new can of soda, its freezing cold bubbles burning all the way down my throat. I pushed the thought of her aside as best I could, straightened up my shoulders and continued walking with a little boost of confident energy in my gait until I reached the table where my friends would gather any minute for lunch.

The uneasiness in my stomach will relax. The traffic jam of pictures in my brain will slow down and disappear. The knot will unravel and I can just chat about what we'll do after school, or the latest reading assignment in English, or the cute boy Mindy bumped into in the lunch line. I can stop the worried tension in my forehead from wrinkling my face from my nose to my eyebrows—that's how it looks to everyone else. To me, it looks like midnight blue and black on the edges. It's a fuzzy, speckled haze of darkness surrounding my insides. The colors squeeze me sometimes so hard that it takes my breath away. Too many colors cluttered together make me troubled, or sometimes confused or worried. I actually can't quite place the feeling exactly. I remind myself that I have it all under control now so that I don't end up back in the hospital again.

As I entered the cafeteria, which was just beginning to teem with eighth graders for third-lunch period, my stomach settled down, and I subtly rolled my shoulders backward a couple of times. I spotted Mindy entering the cafeteria from across the long, busy room. *Melon for Mindy,* I smiled to myself, thinking about the way she always brightens up the mood. I could never wish for a best friend as good to me as she has been.

Mindy walked straight toward me. She was wearing a cantaloupe-colored, long-sleeved tee layered over a celery-green and white-striped tank and straight jeans. I knew it was Mindy. My lips barely turned up; I smiled bigger then, thinking about the way she changes the shade of the room to melon. I noticed she was increasing the speed of her step and waving me closer with the arm that wasn't cradling her notebook in her elbow. The narrowed look in her eyes told me that she had something important to tell me just as those very words mumbled quietly out of her lip-glossed mouth. I leaned forward in anticipation, even though I knew that it was just going to be another one of those issues that appeared more important than it ultimately would turn out to be in the end.

"Vi," she continued waving me close to her face with her free hand. She was bursting with news. "Did you hear that Brittany was dumped by Austin?" she whispered in my ear with sincere disbelief. "I never thought that he'd do it."

"I'm not all that surprised," I said.

"Really? Well," Mindy paused, not sure what she predicted but knowing she was glad of the outcome, "I'm not either. Brittany was always complaining about something. Who wouldn't get sick of that kind of attitude after a while?" Mindy answered her own question. "I mean, she never seemed to be happy, even when there wasn't anything to be unhappy about. He treated her like a star." She shrugged her shoulders and looked in the direction of the growing volume of talk coming from the groups of students entering the cafeteria from the hallway. "That's what I heard, anyway," she added, trying to remove ownership from any gossip she may have uttered.

I nodded my head in agreement for her sake. Brittany was an undercooked pink to me—always an inconsolable sort of person; I figured she liked herself too much to like anyone else. I knew that mindy had a crush on Austin. "Let's go see who else has an opinion about it," I said, and I grabbed Mindy's free arm and turned her back around toward the cafeteria table where a group of girls, and some boys too, would soon sit brimming with their opinions on the newly single Austin. Austin was definitely one of the nicer fourteen-year-old boys around school. He still hadn't realized that he'd eventually be handsome. During the summer, the sun intensified his blond hair while he played baseball and practiced for the football team. He was quite the successful quarterback, according to those who followed the sport.

To me, the boy's "color" was like Mindy's, but with a little more yellow to it. When I see Austin, I think of the chocolates covered in gold foil that my father gives me at Hanukkah, the holiday in December when Jews light the eight candles on the menorah to celebrate a miracle. So Austin has this shiny gold color about him, and this aura seems to easily flow to those around him. I believe that he'll make something of himself someday because of his shiny gold color.

My thoughts were interrupted by the rivers of colors flowing towards me because the table soon would be crammed with other kids. I could hear the volume suddenly rise in the cafeteria as more teens entered. Sitting at long, rectangular tables with round stools attached to them, it's difficult to move around or to talk to more than just whoever was on each side and the two or three people directly on the other side of the table. But these are the times when I have to filter all the thoughts and colors swirling around me. If I could just push away from the table, I might not resent the lack of ability I am given to rest my mind and stretch my legs. Not that my legs are really long. In fact, in comparison, Mindy is a few inches taller than my average height of five feet, barely four inches. But still, I like to have some space of my own. My personal space has always been precious to my stability—my sanity, even. Before anyone sat directly across from me, I pointed my toes and straightened my legs underneath the opposite stool, leaned way back, holding onto the edge of the table and enjoyed my personal space for an extra (fleeting) moment.

The majority of the eighth graders at the table were neither pleased with the gossip about Brittany and Austin nor displeased, but that didn't mean they were indifferent. It is always more interesting to have someone else to talk about so that you weren't the subject of the rumors. I think that this was the reason that most of us passed judgment on each other, because of the fear of being judged. I never heard anyone being totally degrading about whoever the subject of the gossip was, except for maybe some name-calling that was nasty and more false than true. I'd pretend to be interested only so that sometime down the road, I wasn't labeled as one of the ones to be talked about. Not that that was the bravest thing to do. I preferred to lie somewhere between the popular group who seemed to rule the hierarchy—who was cool, who was hot, who was not—and the other cliques that were somewhat more amoebic in size, morphing in shape based on ever-changing interests, friends, and class schedules which determined who would see whom most frequently during the day.

I haven't found myself, so to speak, just yet—I'm not an

athlete, a brain, a skater, goth, or geek. I'm not especially smart or talented at anything in particular. I do well in school because it's important to me, and I like learning about the world around me and my place in it. I want to be somewhere other than this mid-Atlantic town in the middle of Pennsylvania someday. I like music, and my voice holds a tune that gives me some credibility with my peers. I can play the piano too, but I don't play at school. My mother taught me at home, and that was something we did together much like some mothers read books with their kids or fathers toss a ball. I am very grateful for the time Mom played piano and sang beside me; one, because I know there are a lot of children who are ignored by their parents or there is simply little or no time for sharing time doing something fun together; and two, these memories make my heart full. Sitting on the piano bench beside my mother and watching her fingers stretch over the ivory and black keys with barely soundless taps taught me to appreciate the beautiful tone of the instrument and the talent it took to bring its notes to life. She played melodies that streamed a grayish silver color around the room, and once in a while when the tune rose to crescendo as my mother put more pressure on the keys, streaks of white would burst in the air like self-destructing stars. I don't know if it was just the volume of the music increasing or my mother's passion emitting through her performance. I didn't know when I actually started seeing the colors when she played. I just knew that I loved how I felt then— safe, loved, so close to her. I don't feel that way often lately. I miss it.

"Vi, come on. Aren't you hungry?" Mindy was poking my shoulder blade in my back breaking into my reverie to remind me that I was in fact hungry. It was the typical six hours since breakfast, and I hadn't remembered to bring a snack to eat in English class. Ms. Stine allowed us to eat a snack at the start of English class as long as we were quick and discreet with it. She felt that the importance of keeping our brains alert and our stomachs from growling was paramount to the school rule of all food being consumed within the walls of the cafeteria.

I jumped up from the table in a swift mob-like rush to the food line where I grabbed a recycled cardboard tray and a set of plastic silverware wrapped in a flimsy paper napkin and cellophane and stood still for a few seconds as I glossed over the possibilities being offered by our school's attempt at a nutritious yet appealing menu. I decided on the cold fare options, as I usually did, and chose the sliced turkey on a roll as lunch for today. I can never remember to check the lunch menu before I'm actually stuck in the line with no time to spare to make any sort of well-thought out decision about what to eat. I tentatively sniffed a plastic cup that was filled with shredded lettuce and a thin but fresh tomato slice, put it on my tray, and took a packet of mustard to make my sandwich more appetizing. Mindy chose the same sandwich as I did, after making a gagging face towards me when she looked over the other options. She dropped a handful of mayonnaise packets onto her tray, which she then dug into my back to push me along through the line. When I put a bottle of strawberry-flavored water on my tray, she gently pushed her tray into my back again, so I transferred my bottle of water to her tray and took another from the cooler in front of the cashier for myself. We paid and walked back to our table together quickly yet knowing that eyes were probably on us from the other tables who were waiting to be served. Everyone wanted to see what was for lunch while waiting for their turn through the line, unless they packed. I saw a couple girls wrinkle their noses at us and turn their heads in a flip. I reminded myself to not take the snub personally; it was the inconsistent quality, not to mention bland taste, of school cafeteria food, not me who was the object of their obvious scorn. I thought just then of what my father would say to them. It made that smile reappear at the corners of my lips again. My dad always reminds me that when he was in school, there was no choice. You ate what they gave you if you knew what was good for you. He grew up in a classic, conservative suburban town in Massachusetts, so he also reminded me how cold and snowy his long walk to school was while he awaited some warmth from whatever slop was being served when lunch-time finally arrived. Dad didn't think he was being funny, but he was anyway. I laughed inside just thinking of him. It makes me appreciate him more for caring about me so much and making sure that I have more than what I needed. Although what I needed sometimes was Mom. I'd imagine he'd say the same thing.

I ate just about my entire sandwich by the time lunch period was ending. And, I had a better idea of who was on Austin's side and who was on Brittany's side by the end of lunch as well, not that it mattered much to me. Actually, Austin was in my English class this morning, and he didn't appear to be any different from usual. Mindy and I had History together after lunch, so we continued our evaluation of the turkey sandwich and whether Austin will have a new girlfriend by New Year's Eve, which was fast approaching.

"What are you doing after field hockey practice tonight?" I asked Mindy.

"I've got to study for the Algebra test that's on Friday, but other than that...," she left her sentence unfinished and looked at me to determine what I might be asking for beneath the simple question. She pushed the last of her sandwich in her mouth and chewed it in a lump that pushed out her cheek like a squirrel storing a nut too big for its tiny face.

"If you feel like studying at my house, you can come over. Dad won't be home for dinner—it's Wednesday, so...." Mindy knew that Wednesday was the day of the week that my father traveled to Washington, D.C., for work. As an attorney for the state government, it allowed him the flexibility the rest of the week to work in Harrisburg, the capital city of Pennsylvania, to continue the work that he was responsible for with only one long day of travel. I understood this in my fourteen-year-old, mature mind, but since Mom was gone, Wednesdays had become very lonely days for me.

Mom had worked part-time at the flower shop at the mall and taught piano lessons in the afternoons and evenings, but Wednesdays she would set aside her schedule for the two of us. I would try to finish my homework as soon as I arrived home after field hockey practice, if I had it, and then Mom and I would either go out to dinner if she had some extra money, or we'd decide on some dish to try to cook together. The operative word is "try." My mother was average when it came to cooking; she breaded and fried fish on Fridays that Dad and I looked forward to, and she made a few chicken entrees that sufficed in taste and appearance. I started to search the Internet a day or two in advance for something a little out of the ordinary that we both could attempt together.

We made good matzo ball soup even though it was from the box, especially when one of us was sick. And, I remember in particular when we "tried" to make this Italian wedding soup from scratch—we tried a lot of different soup recipes, but we never made any of them twice. None were good enough to bother. I remember Mom said there was some old Yiddish proverb, "Worries go down better with soup." She always seemed to have some lesson about life or some old quote she knew that was appropriate for the situation. She'd tell me not to roll my eyes at her when she'd start using that teaching tone of hers. So the time we tried the Italian wedding soup, we ended up with a baking tray full of tasty tiny baked meatballs and a stockpot full of gelatinous chicken grease and floating escarole. We ate the meatballs plain with the carrots and celery that we hadn't put into the soup with the chicken we were supposed to boil somehow into broth. Then, we played the piano for a little while before bed. Sometimes we'd play and sing for almost two hours without noticing the time flying; other nights, we'd tire after about forty minutes and head up to bed around nine. On those nights, I'd notice that my mother's musical colors weren't as full of white bursts of shimmer as our long nights of song were. Those shorter nights were by no means less meaningful to me and filled my heart just the same, but the silver in the air was a little dull and tinged with a blue fog. The sparkle was missing from my mother's voice and thus in the color I would see. I noticed that my father needed to spend the entire night in D.C. on those nights, and we wouldn't see him till late afternoon on Thursday. I suppose Mom missed him and probably worried about him, and I just felt it, knew it, listened to her thoughts. At that time, I never mentioned to her how I really *saw* it.

"Sure, Violet. In fact, I'll text my mom before practice, and see when she can pick me up from your house later," Mindy said.

"Thanks, Mindy. I appre...."

She cut me off, "I know." We both smiled at each other. Mine was wide, a smile that best friends can have when we trust each other and make concessions for each other like siblings. Maybe even more than for a sibling. Mindy has a younger brother who is six years younger, so she doesn't have much in competition with him in terms of the types of things we do for each other. He's happy if she gives him half of her ice cream sandwich for dessert or lets him play games on her phone.

After History class, Mindy and I headed to the locker room to dress for field hockey practice. I never would have joined the team if it weren't for Mindy. She's quick and determined on the field; she says she'd like the sport to possibly lead towards a scholarship to college one day. I don't doubt it if she continues improving as she has this season. We have one more game this Friday afternoon, and then we're done till next fall. I'm looking forward to the end of the season and spending a little more time on my piano and singing. But, Mindy lives for field hockey season. She joined spring soccer just to keep in shape for field hockey. I admire her commitment to it. Her parents had apparently been good at sports in school themselves, so it's in her genes. Not mine. But, I'm good enough of a runner, and I have enough coordination not to knock out myself or another player with my field hockey stick, so it's been a good way to exercise anyway. Plus, that's how Mindy and I got to be such good friends. We had met having had several classes together, and then she convinced me last year to join the team. I'm not sure if I'll continue on in high school next year. I haven't mentioned that to Mindy just yet.

We rode the bus together at five o'clock to my house. When I'm by myself, I usually just sit by the window to look outside and think about what I can do to make the Wednesday night go by faster while I'm waiting for Dad to come home. It also helps me to ignore the other kids riding the bus home from sports or other activities. Sometimes it's very overwhelming for me being around a large group of people in an enclosed place like a school bus. It makes me want to hold my violet charm close to my breath and see if it changes color—it helps me feel better and in control. I get confused because there feels like there are so many colors mixing around when there are so many different people surrounding me, and that makes me anxious. The knot in my stomach comes back, or my insides squeeze so tight that I feel as if I'm going to choke. I pick up my violet off my chest and hold it up to my breath, and it calms me—long enough to get off the bus or away from the crowd and shake off the confusing colors by closing my eyes and breathing in deeply with my violet clasped in my fingertips just a whisper from my lips. In...out...better.

This Wednesday Mindy and I sat in the third seat behind the driver together. I sat beside the window and glanced out when Mindy paused in her discussion about strategies for the field hockey game on Friday. I was tired and was looking forward to watching some TV, eating some macaroni and cheese or whatever else we felt like making, taking a hot shower and going to bed. But without Mindy, I wouldn't have been as relaxed and looking forward to the evening. Melon Mindy. Better than blue.

We walked right through the foyer to the kitchen when we got to my house, dropped our bags and coats by the desk, and got right to making dinner. I started boiling the water for the macaroni while Mindy made a pitcher of sugar-free lemonade from the little packets of powder in the pantry. She poured each of us a glass, took them into the den and placed them on the coffee table as she picked up the remote for the TV. We watched some new version of teenagers doing what we do at school and each ate half of the box of macaroni and cheese I had made and split into two bowls. Mindy started studying for Friday's math test, and I dug the novel I was reading out of my school bag—*To Kill A Mockingbird*. It really surprises me that more of my classmates don't read books. The stories lift me out of my life much like Alice went to Wonderland and explored a new world. I can imagine myself somewhere else where things haven't happened to me yet but can. It's hard for me not to be carried away by books. I especially like to delve into them to pass the time I used to fill with my mother.

Mindy was picked up at 8 o'clock. I thanked her for keeping me company once again; she gave me a hug good night, and I watched as she ran with her bags towards the street where her mother was waiting in their car. Both of them waved to me as Mindy opened the back door to throw her school bag and field hockey stuff into the back. I yelled "bye" as cheerfully as I could muster and closed the front door. I looked up the stairwell and decided to shower and wait in bed for dad to come home. Practice had worn me out as the December weather was growing colder and making it much harder to stay warm even while running up and down the field. With quiet feet, I dragged myself up the stairs and undressed in my bathroom with the water beginning to steam the room. The clouds of white reminded me of the silver of my mother and her music. I tried not to cry at first, but I stepped gingerly into the hot shower and let my tears go.

Her first note to me was on a sheet of fine stationery paper folded neatly in half, a pale violet:

My Little Violet,
Plant some flowers in the yard to remember that life must sometimes weather storms, but they need the warmth of sunshine and the drench of rain if you ever expect to find the rainbows.

Chapter 2

DAD had come home around ten, shortly after I had climbed into my bed. I love my bed; it is a double and the headboard and frame was once my grandparents'. My mother had slept in it growing up, and now it is mine. No doubt I love it more because of that fact alone. The wood is painted like butter with a trim around the edges the color of gingerbread. I've had the same quilt for years now even though Mom had offered to replace it last Christmas. I suppose it looks rather girlish, but I'm not ready to part with the tiny violets and mint leaves on the soft creamy cotton. I was never fond of the short, stiff ruffles around its edges because it made it look old-fashioned, but now I think it looks sophisticated. No one else I know has such a precious heirloom to treasure.

On my ninth birthday, my mother and father let me decorate my room myself, and I had no difficulty deciding upon the quilt with little violets, like me—Little Violet. After we brought it home with matching linens and a few small round pillows that remind me of nonpareils, those round milky pastel chocolates dotted with white beads of sugar sprinkled on top of its baby curl, my mother smoothed out the wrinkles and lay back on the bed with her hands clasped behind her head. She closed her eyes, and with a dreamy smile on her face, she said, "Your bedroom should be your palace, where you are most at peace."

Ever since then, I have always been able to feel a little closer to her once I enter my bedroom and prepare for sleep. The picture of her in my head when she said those words to me is vivid; the way her voice sounded is beginning to fade. I don't even want to admit that to myself, but it's true. I've tried to call her cell phone from mine, only to be met with a recorded message from the phone company that the number has been disconnected. As much as I've been mad at her for not trying to contact me or Dad after all this time, I still wish she would. I'm still skeptical about why Mom left and where she is and why I've not heard from her—except for the note.

I looked at the small framed photograph on my nightstand of Mom when she was about my age, sitting on my bed; of course it was hers at the time. I can barely see the tones of the wood headboard behind her long coffee brown hair pulled behind a headband. Her knees are pulled up to her chest, and she is resting her chin on her knees, head tilted to the right which makes her gaze slightly off center. She was wearing denim shorts and some summery white top that set off her dark hair even more. I continue to wonder what she was thinking in that picture because her position is relaxed, at peace she might say, but her eyes look occupied with something else—something more important than a teenager would summarily daydream about while sitting on her bed.

I heard Dad trying to quietly close the door to the house as he entered from the garage. If he would just grease the hinges to the door, he wouldn't have to try so hard to close it quietly. It's hard to know whether to push it shut quickly and hopefully avoid the screech of metal against metal or to hold it tightly and push it inch by inch closer to the doorjamb with a final shove. Just by listening, I know Dad is tensing his neck muscles and pressing his teeth together without realizing that he is. I felt a wave of Tiffany blue coming up the stairs as my father crept up to check to see if I was still awake, even though he knows that most likely I was. Even in my palace, sleep still takes its time arriving until, in my mind, everyone else I know is resting deeply.

"You're still awake, Violet?" Dad asked with his tender brown eyes and voice that conveyed no surprise in his question.

"How was your day, Dad? Traffic okay?" I asked. Dad gets agitated with the time he wastes in the car between work and home only because he can't do anything constructive. I've tried to tell him that he should cherish the quiet and the excuse to do nothing for an hour and a half or so. That's not his personality though, to waste time listening to quiet and doing nothing but driving.

He walked over to me in bed, tugged at my hair and kissed me on the forehead. I slid over to make room for him to sit beside me. Even in my double bed, I always sleep on the left side closest to my nightstand and my mother's picture. Dad sat down with an audible exhale. Tiffany blue puffed in the air but lime green followed. He missed her.

"Busy. Work and traffic. I think with the holidays approaching, everyone becomes consumed by getting around as fast as possible with no regard for others. Where has common courtesy gone?" he shook his head side to side. He ran his left index finger across the top of Mom's head in my picture frame. He quickly turned his face back to me and tugged my hair again. "How was your day? Did Mindy come over after practice?"

I nodded. "We made macaroni, did some homework in front of the TV. Same as usual."

"Nothing wrong with the usual. It gives us, um," he looked back at Mom's picture to choose the right word, "harmony." Dad seemed content as he rose from my bed and walked over to my window. He pulled the string of the linen Roman shade to look out into the darkness, and I could see his green reflection in the glass. Before the moonlight could find its way into my bedroom, my father pulled the string again and let the shade fall closed to the sill. "Good night, Violet. Sleep tight."

"Night, Dad. Love you."

"I love you too, sweetheart. See you in the morning." He walked over to me lying in bed, my quilt up to my chin, and kissed me quickly on the top of my head without meeting my eyes. I'm sure his were beginning to fill up with uncomfortable tears that he wanted to let go of but not in front of me.

As Dad closed my bedroom door, I remained sitting up in bed for a moment, unmoving and gazing after him. I was pretty sure that I wasn't going to be able to fall asleep right away. Reminders of my mother inched into my brain even as I tried to fall asleep. I tried to fight them off because I know it's a school night, and our last game is Friday night, so I wanted to stockpile some rest. I paused another ten seconds even though I knew I wasn't going to stay under my quilt. I had to sing Mom a song first.

I pushed down the quilt with my feet and grabbed my field hockey sweatshirt that was hanging over my desk chair. With the energy that music gives me, I pulled the navy blue Cobalt Valley Cavaliers sweatshirt over my head and twisted it down over my heather gray sweatpants and tee shirt that served as my pajamas. Walking through the dark hallway, I banged my elbow into the wall. I didn't stifle my "ouch" as there was no sense in trying not to awaken Dad as he probably wasn't asleep yet anyway. He very well may have been listening for my descent downstairs to the piano and would have been surprised, if not disturbed, if he didn't hear my footsteps patter down the hall. Playing piano at night was a habit—bad or good, I couldn't say.

I rubbed my right elbow with the opposite hand and tried to be more careful. I turned left at the bottom of the stairs into what Mom and I called "the parlor." We were trying to sound elite, and I still laugh when I call the room this luxurious name instead of the living room or den like other people would. Even so, I feel overtaken by elegance when I sit on the dark walnut piano bench and feel its smoothness with my palms as I slide it across the hardwood floor towards the instrument. Mom's piano is an upright, not remarkably expensive or refined or well-named in any way, but she kept it in tune and free of dust and fingerprints. I think it belonged to someone in her family but never knew exactly who it was. One of the books of music that we played from the most was already set up on the case, but I didn't need to look at the notes on the page. The song was in my head, my ears, my heart. The finish of the upright is so polished that the walnut grain is almost violet in places. The instrument overflows with color and sound, encasing me in a bubble as if I'm somewhere other than the parlor of my house. The room is empty of anything but deliberate pitches of notes swimming together in melodies. They are sweet to my ear from my fingertips to my tongue as the tune spills out of my lips. When I finished the final chord, a rainbow of colors disappeared before I have even opened my eyes to see it.

Fewer than ten minutes has passed from my descent to the parlor, and I make a pit stop in the kitchen for a glass of water from the tap. Satisfied with my playing, even solo, I knew that Mom would be proud. I can't always play with such definitiveness, and there have been more times that I leave the piano with the song unfinished because I start to cry—missing my mother and wanting her to hear my playing—than times that I am satisfied; but tonight my hands were confidently brushing over the keys and drawing softness and volume when the song required it. I was pleased and therefore able to go to bed feeling fulfilled, finally tired from the day.

I took my glass of water with me and set it on my bedside table in front of my mother's picture like a liquid mirror, the glass reflecting her colors, her shades of purple still visible to me. I smiled at her in the dimness of my room knowing that she was by my side. *I miss you.*

I awoke to a bright yellow day full of promise. I wanted to read some more of *To Kill A Mockingbird* before English class this morning, so I put on jeans, sneakers, and a pale yellow long-sleeved tee over my gray camisole to match the mood of the day to come. While I brushed my teeth in the bathroom and smoothed my hair back in a ponytail, I saw my violet around my neck in the mirror. It had specks of yellow spiraling through the petals. It should be a good day. I smiled with optimism—nothing wrong with feeling alert and ready for a good day.

While I ate half a ruby red grapefruit sprinkled with sugar at the kitchen table and tried to get further into the novel, Dad shuffled in from the squeaky side door that leads to the garage with his cup of black coffee and today's newspaper.

"Brrr…it's definitely starting to feel like winter out there!"

I nodded. "If you'd put on a coat and shoes instead of running outside in your robe and bare feet, maybe it wouldn't freeze your toes off." I sounded like my mom.

Dad laughed. He raised his favorite oversized coffee mug in the air and said, "Who needs shoes when you have hot coffee?!" Even Dad could feel the positive forces set out for the day. He released more black coffee into his mug from the coffee dispenser, Mom's gift to him on his last birthday. I had given him a couple pounds of his favorite coffee blend. Then, he sat down comfortably next to me at the kitchen table and unfolded the front section of the paper.

We read silently for a solid fifteen minutes until it was time for me to brave the cold at the bus stop at the corner of Crest and Hillside in front of our neighbor's house. Many of the homes in our neighborhood were ranch homes, three-bedrooms and a single-car garage, built in the 70s. Ours is one of the few two-stories; it has a sandy-colored brick front with brown aluminum siding around the back. The windows aren't as large as I would like; it's always so much nicer when the natural light can brighten the house. We have hardwood floors in decent condition in the foyer and parlor that run right through the dining room and kitchen. The rooms are small but certainly cozy and enough for us. Carpet that reminds me of the creamy coffee that Mom drank flows from the edge of the hardwood in the front hall up the stairs and back through the three bedrooms. The first room on the right is mine, next to the bathroom. Dad sleeps at the opposite end of the hall from my room in the bedroom that my parents once shared. The middle room has changed purposes throughout the years. It was once the nursery for my crib and baby dresser; it was a craft room for a while when my Mom thought she would try out scrapbooking, needlepoint, quilting—she always fell back to her music. There is a treadmill in there now, although I would guess the machine itself travelled more miles from Sears to this room than it has seen since.

Our neighbor's house is also a two-story. I've never been inside but its layout appears to be similar as far as I can tell from the outside. As I passed the house on my way to the corner where the street sign marks the bus stop, it strikes me that the colors from our house were mixed with a little purple to make a taupe-colored brick and a mushroom shade surrounding the sides of our neighbor's. I could take a tour of the house to see its insides now that it's up for sale. Just last weekend the widow who lived there was moved out by her son and daughter into a retirement community in Florida. She was one of those lively, aging women who likes to stay busy and has more of a social life than many younger people because she doesn't have to go to school or work all day. Apparently, her children were concerned about the upkeep of the house, so it was time for a move. She was very excited; one morning last week while I was waiting for the school bus, she told me about the new condo she'll be living in when she came out front to the sidewalk to pick up her morning newspaper. There are two swimming pools, a social club, tennis courts, even a beauty salon and a coffee shop, right in the community, she told me. It must be nice to look forward to a life where every day started such a sunny yellow.

I haven't noticed anyone house hunting next door, but that

doesn't count for much as I'm not around during the day. For the size and age of the houses in our neighborhood, they don't typically stay empty for long. Maybe I'll check it out this weekend if I notice a realtor and potential buyers poking around. I enjoy walking through empty houses and imagining living there, placing furniture at particular angles, and pretending that it's mine.

The sound of the bus's brakes squealing broke into my musings about what Mrs. Suden's house must have looked like inside what with everything gone. I shifted my backpack higher on my left shoulder and watched the bus approach the corner. Only when it came to a complete stop, as Mom always warned me about, I started my steps towards the folding door. It opened, and I happened to glance back at my house; surprisingly, Dad's face was in the kitchen window with his big coffee mug held up to his chin. I didn't have the presence of mind to wave or smile, not even knowing if he'd be able to see my gesture. But, the melded blue-green rays streaming from the window told me that he was trying hard to push his sadness aside and concentrate on work. I sat down on the bench seat and slid over next to the window and was able to see Dad drop his head to his chest in a quick motion, then inhale deeply and straighten up as if he knew I wanted to see him pull himself together and take on the day with strength of mind.

Mindy came by my locker on her way to homeroom. I was trying to stuff my winter coat inside along with my backpack and my bag with some of my field hockey practice gear. It wasn't fitting very well. I should have just taken my field hockey clothes straight to the locker room.

Mindy was as melon as ever this morning. She was chattering away before she even got close enough for me to hear her over the conversations of others in the hallway.

"Vi, can you believe that Alexis got her phone taken again?! Already this morning!" Here we go with the newscast of the day.

I took a couple notebooks and my novel out of my backpack while Mindy filled me in with details that I'm sure were a conglomeration of different versions she heard somewhere between Facebook and the front door of the school. I finally squeezed the fluff of my coat in my locker underneath my backpack, which I hadn't emptied completely of its contents, and my practice stuff. It's a good thing that field hockey was almost over so I could start securing my locker better and finding my books. We walked around the corner in front of the library around to homeroom. I had Ms. Stine, who was also my English teacher, while Mindy had Mr. Matthews, the science teacher, further down the hall. I liked Ms. Stine, probably because I also liked English class. Science class was fun sometimes, but I don't always like to smell and look at all the jarred lab animals and other stuff that was once alive. I don't know if it was the untidiness of science class that made me feel chaotic inside, not bad; it just was hard to clear my head in there. And, Mr. Matthews was a good teacher, too, which made me feel sort of disloyal because I didn't like the subject as much as other classes. I feel pretty lucky with the teachers I've had so far in Cobalt Valley. I never doubted that my future would include college, and I think that I have liked more teachers than I haven't, so that's promising.

"Good morning, Violet." Ms. Stine greeted me personally most mornings unless I beat her to it.

Mindy said her last words to me before she'd see me at lunch later on today. "Hi, Ms. Stine," Mindy said and gave a little wave to me while she quickened her steps to catch up to a couple of girls on the field hockey team headed her way.

"Hi, Ms. Stine," I repeated my friend's words and walked past my teacher into the room to my seat in the row closest to the windows. The school's TV studio broadcast of the announcements was scrolling today's day, date and greeting on top of a sunny yellow background. Kind of ironic. I opened up my novel and started to reread the last couple of paragraphs where I had stopped this morning at breakfast. I spent homeroom reading while listening to the announcements and trying to block out some of my classmates who must not have the Algebra test that I have tomorrow or any other homework that was pressing. Homeroom extends into first period, which is for activities; I have chorus on four days of the six-day cycle and a study hall two days out of the six. I won't play piano for the school, just at home. I'm kind of embarrassed when I play because it feels so personal to me. The band director bugs me about joining though. I try to avoid him when I go over to the music wing of the school. I just told him I didn't have any room in my schedule, and it was hard to keep track of the cycle day anyway. The school year runs on six-day cycles so that we don't miss classes due to vacation days that fall on weekdays. It makes sense, I suppose. Sometimes we shuffle around in a disorganized mess after a long vacation though.

I was glad that I had time this morning to read further in my book. I was just finally getting into the characters; it was hard at first to get used to the dialect used in the South in the 60s. I want sometimes to be as tough as the main character Scout seems to be, but I've never been a tomboy or had to stick up for myself much, on the playground and stuff like that. I wonder if she'll change. I don't think people really change; they can make decisions that show that they're compromising their values or treat others in ways that they regret afterwards, but deep inside, I think that people are who they are because of some combination of nature and nurture—how they were born and how they were raised—maybe a little more of one and less of the other. I think it might depend on the parents. Like me. Like Mindy. *Like you, Mom.*

Before I knew it, it was time for English class. I was really glad because my stomach was growling so noisily I was sure that everyone within arm's reach could hear it, like a little bear aching for its honey. I took the oatmeal and chocolate chip cereal bar that

I had brought, and continued reading while I tore open the foil wrapper and nibbled off a chewy bite. It didn't take but a minute for my little bear to stop its growling and settle down for an interesting English class.

It seemed as if Ms. Stine also felt like it was a sunny yellow day. "Good morning, everyone. Finish your journal entry for today and get ready to go back in time today. We're going back to the 60s to find some insight into the setting of *To Kill A Mockingbird*."

Ms. Stine captured my attention with her opening. I don't think that I was the only one either. Austin who sat to my right also seemed to nod his head in an intrigued motion. He's rather yellow to me most days, even gold, because he's so smart and confident. He's easy to like. He was eating a protein bar that looked like some mixture of strawberry and vanilla. He rested it in between his teeth while he dug around in his backpack for his copy of the novel.

We worked in a large group that class period and made a human timeline. Each of us was given an event in history surrounding the setting of the novel, and we had to use our knowledge and educated guesses to put them in order. We clearly didn't know much about the excessive lack of equal rights that existed in the South during that time. It's quite surprising that it really wasn't so long ago. I noticed a few of my classmates discussing something with Ms. Stine that seemed to be agitating her. It must be hard to teach about this type of topic—it could be painful for some, confusing, yet fascinating at the same time.

Ms. Stine concluded, "If we don't learn from history, we are bound to repeat it." She acknowledged that this was a cliché but that it rang true as a theme from this book. "Think for a couple minutes about another example that supports this notion and share it with a classmate. Write a summary of both of your examples and turn it in for your writing assignment for the day. Then, you may read for the remainder of the class period."

My first thought was about my mother. I feel as if I want to appreciate every moment of my life, which I know is also an over-used notion, to make the absence of my mother feel meaningful. I've learned from her early departure, but I didn't think it was something that Austin would really want to discuss, even briefly, on such an upbeat day.

Austin made it easy on me. He said, "World War II. The Nazis. They targeted the Jews. That's the same kind of discrimination that this book is talking about, don't you think?"

"Oh, definitely. I hadn't thought of that one."

"And, the Civil War. The slaves were the target of the racism then," Austin continued.

"Let's use your two examples. How'd you think of them so quickly?" I asked with honest admiration, not just relief that I wouldn't have to share what exactly I was thinking about.

Austin gave a wry smile. "I actually like history. I watch the History Channel at night when I can't sleep," he said. After a moment, he added, as if he wasn't sure he could trust me with that personal information, "And when there isn't something going on sports-wise that I have to check out." He looked down at his summary on his desk and tapped his pen against the side of his head. I think he was wondering whether I believed his last statement as much as I knew his first was the real truth. He flashed me one quick smile, and then we both returned to the writing on our desks and our novels for the period.

"Thanks for the great answers," I offered without meeting his eyes.

"Anytime," Austin said, as he stretched his legs out in front of him and held his paper up with his long, agile arms so that I could see he hadn't written much.

He is a good guy, I thought. He'll definitely go far in life and make a fine husband someday. For someone else.

Walking into the cafeteria for lunch was like approaching a sunset. The sunny yellow day had tinges of pink and red and orange filtering through my vision as if the room's walls were being washed with watercolors. One of the walls of the cafeteria was entirely windows which let in the bright blue sky free of clouds and created the mood in here—the yellow day I sensed from this morning. As we entered from various hallways that led away to the 8th grade wing, the music hall, and the main lobby, the shades of the sunset seeped in as well. Anger at a friend. Frustration at failing a test. Hunger and fatigue. I shuddered slightly as I walked into the room with my bag and books. Large crowded rooms take away my peace.

Because I had had some extra time this morning getting ready, I had managed to throw together some turkey on a multigrain bagel and a large sour green apple. While I was looking for Mindy, I stopped at the convenience machine to slide in my dollar for a lemon water. As it chugged down the chute into the well at the bottom, I heard some commotion near the other side of the cafeteria. Ms. Stine, Mr. Houseman, the principal, and another teacher whom I couldn't make out from my distance were shouting at a couple of students to stop. I didn't have to use any extraordinary ability to know it wasn't to stop eating or stop trying to do homework during lunch.

Mr. Houseman had one boy by the elbow and was dragging him towards the office through the cafeteria. He kept turning back and giving Ms. Stine and the other boy an evil look.

"It's not fair!" he kept repeating.

Ms. Stine didn't move. Her arms crossed, she stared right back at the boy, straight in the eye, with an unswayable glare of disdain. I never knew her to stand for liars much.

The other teacher, who taught math I think, walked the other boy out to the music hallway which invariably led to the office too. A good guess would be that we wouldn't see those two for five to ten school days depending upon the seriousness of their offenses.

I knew it wouldn't be tough to know the full story once I found

Mindy. I have to ignore the mountains of speculation that swell around me at times like these; otherwise, I would start feeling panic coming on. I saw Mindy already halfway through the lunch line chatting away with a boy who looked like he had some kind of pertinent information about the previous fight. Either that or he was enjoying Mindy's attention. His white golf shirt was turning orange ever so slightly; it reminded me of orange sherbet, but more importantly, he had a crush on Mindy as far as I could tell.

"Clay said that they're always trying to kill each other," Mindy began as she approached me without bothering with a greeting. She sat down next to me at our regular table already gulping a soda. She set a tray carrying a slice of pizza and a side salad in front of her. "Over stupid stuff." She folded the slice in her palm and took a bite, satisfied with her update.

I wrapped up the last bits of my sandwich and started eating my apple. The juice of the fruit made my mouth water and my cheeks snap with the sourness. Just then Clay sauntered over to our table and hesitated before he evaluated whether he was welcome to sit down. Mindy gave him permission with a smile and a beckoning wave. I said hello to him; he returned the greeting with a smile that lasted a little longer than I had anticipated considering he seemed interested in Mindy, not me. While he was offering us his estimation of the previous event at lunch, I couldn't help thinking of orange sherbet.

Clay always pretends to have a French accent; he reminds me of Steve Martin in the movie *The Pink Panther*. I never saw the whole movie or anything, because it's really old. But, I remember seeing parts of it somewhere. But, Clay is just like the absent-minded inspector who's actually kind of funny in a peculiar sort of way. I'm never sure whether I should take him seriously or not. "Mademoiselle Stine, whatever are we going to do with thees een-appropriate behavior?!" He paused and emphasized the appropriate syllables with grand arm gestures.

Ms. Stine walked by our table as she monitored proper decorum in the cafeteria. She nodded to Clay with a small smile at his humor.

Clay shook his head and stroked his chin appearing as if he was seriously contemplating solving the crime. Suddenly, he raised his index finger in the air as if he had a bright idea. "Ah ha!" Some other students nearby turned around at the volume of his epiphany. "Ze culprit is ze one who threw ze second punch. He was ze one who had to have started it weeth hees beeg mouth."

We all laughed. Ms. Stine continued her lunchtime stroll. It really didn't matter to us what they were fighting about. In eighth grade, it's about time that boys, and girls for that matter, should have learned that fighting doesn't solve the problem. Really. Grow up.

Mindy finished her slice of pizza and salad while Clay was giving her his full attention. She and I were discussing what we'd like to do after our last field hockey game tomorrow night. I think he wanted to know where Mindy would be every minute, but by sticking around during our conversation, he'd at least know where we'd be the majority of Friday evening. Clay surprised me when he put his elbow on the table and was just resting his jaw on his knuckles staring at Mindy, when it was time to head to our last class. We gathered our books and trays on our way out of the cafeteria into the hallway towards History class, which Mindy and I had together. It was the only class we actually had at the same time, although we both had a lot of the same subjects.

A group of girls was still seated at one of the tables near the exit of the cafeteria. Ms. Stine was standing nearby them talking to the other teacher who had helped break up the fight earlier. The sunny yellow of the room was darkened over there as if a pink sun was setting over the horizon into a deep fiery red. Someone was mad. It squeezed my chest as I was making my way through the crowds heading to class. A burst of emotion pushed me into Mindy as I walked between Ms. Stine and the table of girls.

One of the girls was talking loudly enough to be heard over the layer of noise that is always covering the cafeteria. I was sure that the teachers could hear her if they had a mind to.

"I hate her class. It's stupid. She talks about the 60s. Who cares?" No one else was responding to the girl ranting; in fact, they were mostly looking down at the table or their trays or at the clock on the far wall. It was a peculiar shade of pink we were passing through—red and yellow streaks. I didn't know her. The girl talking, I mean. But, I recognized her because she had been hanging around the field during field hockey practice a couple weeks ago. The coach asked her to leave because she was distracting, talking about girls on the team as if they weren't there, as if they wouldn't hear her jabs at them. She was another kind of fighter, I'd say. Nasty words. But she wouldn't stand behind them. She took them back as soon as they flew out of her mouth.

"I never said that." She said *that* a lot. It's fair then, I guess; Ms. Stine probably dislikes that girl for being a liar, just as much as that girl hates the teacher for being so boring and taken with the past.

I remembered her clutching a bright pink notebook. She was sitting on the bleachers listening to her iPod and writing in it. A Slam Book, I guessed, being passed around from one person to the next like a journal of notes. It's easier to fool the teachers than writing and passing notes to each other, if the notes are in a notebook. After practice, she was complimenting us girls on what a great practice we had. It was hard not to be appreciative because she was so positive, but at the same time, Mindy and I were questioning her intent. I brushed it off because I didn't know her well enough to think she was insincere. I typically give people the benefit of the doubt. And it's definitely encouraging to receive random admiration. I'd forgotten about it till now. I wondered if Mindy recalled it. The whole thing seemed insignificant at the time, and I'd never noticed her before.

As everyone was preparing to exit the cafeteria, I saw the loud-mouthed girl lean over the table and snatch the same notebook I had remembered from the middle of another girl's pile of books cradled in her crossed arms. All of the innocent girl's books tumbled out of her grasp as she barely looked up through her eyelashes at the one who yanked it from her. The notebook was as pink as the puff of air around their table. Red darts shot right through me, and I jumped sideways, even though I knew they weren't real once I thought about it clearly. No one else could see them, nor would they even harm me. The vision felt like stabs in my head—these girls being so mean and phony towards each other. I didn't see a whole story unfold, but I pushed my fingers into my eyelids trying to relieve the headache that was erupting.

I was too far past the table to help the girl retrieve her books, but a couple of the others next to her helped her pile them back up so that they could make their way to class. Although somewhat subtle, I could tell that they were intimidated. I hoped for a brief moment that they didn't let that girl push them around. But after all, she was good at dishing out the nice words too. I just wondered whether the friendships were a matter of convenience to her. It seemed like she was more of a chameleon, that little lizard that changes its colors to match the environment in order to save itself from harm. It made me wonder what her name was and why she was so disingenuous towards Ms. Stine.

The flow of eighth graders ebbed out of the cafeteria in a rhythm of movement and chatter that began to decrescendo as we entered the classroom doors and settled in to our afternoon classes. Mindy and I walked in to History without my getting the chance to point out that girl to her to see whether Mindy remembered her from field hockey practice that one day. As the lecture of the day started, I forgot about it for the time being. But I'd learn the girl's name soon enough whether I liked it or not.

The next note from Mom was written on orange paper the color of gerber daisies, that creamy mango hue:

My Little Violet,
Be patient. Not everyone knows what you know. You may not even know it yet either.

Chapter 3

MINDY and I had our last field hockey practice this afternoon after school to get ready for our last game tomorrow night. Keeping in tune with the color of the day, practice went off pretty successfully. We warmed up and ran the drills to maintain our endurance during the game. I'm always impressed by the ease with which Mindy plays. It's as if the stick is an extension of her body; it never seems to get in her way or move unintended. She usually plays offense while I usually play defense, but it depends upon the other team's strengths and experience to determine which positions we play. I know that this is more than a game to her; it is her ticket out of here, to college. Field hockey is very popular in Central Pennsylvania, and several local colleges scout our high school. Even if I play my personal best, no college is going to offer me a scholarship in this sport or any other. I've got to get there on my own talents, which I haven't quite figured out yet.

I was really looking forward to arriving home after practice and making quick headway to bed. Tomorrow night was our last game, and the sooner I slept the night away, the sooner it would be over and the end of another season. I guess I'll see whether Mindy can convince me to play again next year, but I'm ready to have some more time to practice piano, sing, read, think, for now anyway. I'm not so sure I'll play unless Mindy gives me a hard time about it, although I'd be disappointed if our friendship would suffer from not spending as much time together.

For now, I did have to study just a little bit for the test in Algebra tomorrow. Without studying, it was a sure way for a C (or worse) to crop up on my report card. Algebra just didn't come easy to me like English did. Math is another thing I couldn't wait to finish, but I've resigned myself to the knowledge that I had to face it for quite a number of years in school yet, since college was definite.

Mindy hitched a ride home with another girl on the team who lived near her. Mindy and I actually don't spend a whole lot of time with her anymore. Her name is Stacey. Mindy has known her almost her entire life since they live a few houses away from each other. She's one of those friendships that was forced as a neighbor but as Mindy and Stacey grew up, they grew apart. That's also the time that Mindy and I grew closer and became better friends. I never knew what exactly came between them, because Mindy was always more of her friend than I had ever been. But, Stacey just sort of became that annoying kind of a person who wanted to do only what she wanted to do, and after a while, that type of person isn't much of a friend. I said good-bye to Mindy as she climbed into Stacey's mother's car, one of those sporty SUV's in a pretty, sparkling oyster color, which made me feel as if Stacey was covering up something, even if she wasn't really. Stacey never did anything mean to me; it was just a feeling I had when she was around. But that happens to me a lot, and I can't usually make sense of it.

I psyched myself up for the ride home on the late bus by toying with the violet around my neck. I slid it side to side on its cord just barely brushing it across my lips. It's almost as if electricity sparked between it and my body. I waited with some of the girls from the field hockey team while the athletes from basketball practice and lifting and working out in the gym were finishing up. Huddles of us would be vying for seats on the busses. No one in particular makes me nervous; it's just the whole enormity of it. All the people. All the voices. All the colors. I tried to focus on the calm colors that I saw in between all of the deepest hues of red, blue, and especially black. I inhaled deeply and exhaled so that my breath coated my violet along with my fingertips. And I closed my eyes for a moment to help me focus again. It's as if everyone was asking me questions all at once, and I can't answer them. I took another couple of breaths while everyone was making his or her way towards the bus door. I felt like there was an ocean current forcing me along, and I couldn't catch my breath. They were pushing me under, but no one knew it nor could help me from suffocating. I was beginning to panic inside. I either had to dart ahead and make my way through the group that was forming the line entering the bus, or I had to break away from the crowd to get some air. And then I couldn't assure myself a window seat that helped me endure the bus ride home. I didn't know what to do. And I didn't know how I was going to figure it out before the oxygen left my body for good. I couldn't even worry about what everyone was going to think—it was that bad. I looked down towards the ground, away from the people, the colors. I was still holding onto my violet, much more tightly than I had realized. Someone next to me laid a hand on my arm and asked me if I was all right. I kept my gaze on the ground and nodded.

"Are you sure?" the voice said.

The world around me seemed to become silent. That voice echoed in my ears. My heartbeat must have disguised the sound for it sounded like my mother. I felt like I was straining to hear the music. But there couldn't have been any playing.

"Violet?" The hand shook me gently.

Suddenly, I could hear again as gold filtered into my vision, and Austin was looking at me with an earnest intensity. He held me firmly by the arm and led me up the three steps of the bus pushing me down into the first available seat on our left. He sat down right next to me, took my bag off my arm so that he could make us more comfortable in the double seat that is somehow supposed to be big enough for growing teenagers and kindergarteners alike.

I had trouble finding my voice; I just looked at him. It must've looked like I was glaring at him because he met my gaze and then faced forward and said, "Sorry if I hurt your arm, but you looked like you were gonna faint or throw up or something."

I stuttered a bit, mostly because I didn't really know what I was going to say to Austin, but I reassured him by moving my face close enough to his where he had to turn to look at me. "I...I...I get lightheaded when I feel trapped in a crowd. It's a phobia, I guess."

He nodded without surprise or judgment. "My mom hates travelling on airplanes. Similar kind of a thing, I think." He shrugged his shoulders and laid his head back against the seat. He propped his knees up on the seat in front of us, his sneakers brushing against the gym bag on the floor that he must have brought for practice after school, being the athlete that he was.

"Well, I appreciate your help anyway." I hoped I sounded as sincere as I felt. The more I thought about it, I was certain that Austin saved me from what could've been one of my most embarrassing moments ever. "Thank you. Austin, I mean it. Thank you."

"It's cool. Glad I was there." He closed his eyes, and I was sure I saw a hint of smile appear just as he relaxed himself for the bus ride home. There still seemed to be gold dust floating in the air around him. I was sure that he didn't see that.

I leaned my own head back against the seat and smiled as I looked out the window and saw that we were almost home. I breathed in deep even breaths and rolled my violet between my thumb and index finger skimming my chin with it so that I could feel its coolness. I laid it on my chest and sensed its clarity of color, the clearing of the purple in its petals.

I needed to ask my mother to help me understand how I can

stop the feeling of panic that overtakes me. How can I control something that feels so out of my control? Even more distressing is why throngs of people bother me so. It's not as if I'm in an unfamiliar place or with kids that don't share the same hallways and classrooms with me all day. I should feel content when I'm here on the bus or at school. When we travel to another school for a field hockey game, I have always had a few tremors of uncertainty, which I can mask as nervousness about the game. The company of my teammates around me and the freedom of the outside air should make the anxiety go away. But it doesn't. Not always. Sometimes the colors surrounding us mix with the fresh clear air, so they're less intense. The healthy energy that is essential to our hockey game dissipates as we run around the field. I see the colors round and pound into each other's space and away from the competitive edge when an opponent gets too close. I don't cheat by trying to use their thoughts to anticipate my next move. Sometimes the air steams with red, passion and determination; gold, conviction and direction; a silvery orange, vitality and power. But, that feeling you get when you know someone is right behind you, yet you can't see them—that's how I feel a lot, that's violet.

I gave Austin a friendly shove on his shoulder as I climbed over his knees to get out of the bus seat and off the bus when we arrived at my corner. "See ya," I said.

He opened his eyes without at all seeming startled and waved his hand in the air just as I glanced back and smiled and went down the steps and out the door. I slid my bag up over my shoulder and stood still for a moment to watch the bus depart. It accelerated with volume and the smell of exhaust, so I held my breath till it passed. I shivered a bit as the chill in the air was colder than on the bus. Winter is here. Or maybe I felt a little better now, off the bus.

I started walking home passing the For Sale sign in front of Mrs. Suden's house and continuing down the sidewalk in front of our yard. I was thinking about spending a little time before dinner playing the piano. It makes me calm down after a panic attack like I had. Had Mom been home, she would've asked me how my day was, and I could've shared with her what happened to me before getting on the bus to go home. She would've suggested that we start something for dinner and then sit at the piano together and play. The contrast of the white and black keys would heal my need for balance. The melodies would release my thoughts and craft peaceful colors. I would stop worrying about whatever it was that always seemed to be just beyond reach.

I hadn't realized that I was looking at the ground while I was walking, concentrating on my feet and the cracks in the walk instead of what was in front of me. That's how I ran right into Cropsie. When I realized what I had done, the words "Excuse me," seemed so inappropriate, but I said them anyway as I zigzagged around the old man and jetted across my yard to our house. Cropsie lives down Crest Road four or five blocks on the opposite side of the street. I couldn't help but to glance back at him to make sure that he was still walking down the street and away from me, his shadow getting smaller as he was further from my view. I don't know how Cropsie got his name or reputation, but he reminds me of the spooky neighbor Boo Radley in *To Kill A Mockingbird* that Scout and her brother dare each other to taunt. Early in the book, all Scout's brother Jem is able to do is run up to the Radley house, touch it, and run back out the gate, for fear of this man with a weird look in his eye who barely comes outside except to scare young children. Cropsie is like the mysterious Radley man because we were as frightened of him as we were intrigued by him, just as Scout and Jem were. At Halloween, when it was time to make our rounds through the neighborhood, we worked ourselves so scared of him, even though we had never seen his face. It was this tempting curiosity—wanting to see what he looked like but being too scared to approach the house. I'm not sure what he'd ever done, if anything, to warrant the status in the neighborhood he has, but I've never had the courage to ask him or the interest to discuss it with anyone else. I imagine it would be an interesting story if I would bring it up; the topic of him doesn't seem to arise in ordinary conversation, however. So, I just avoid him.

I unlocked the front door rather quickly, trying not to appear hurried or nervous, pushed the door open and closed in one fluid motion, and locked it behind me. I dropped my bag by the door and took off my jacket. Walking to the coat closet, I could see through the front window blinds and saw Cropsie's lurching stride continuing down the sidewalk. I slowed my breathing to a regular pattern without realizing it had increased with anxiety yet again. I actually laughed out loud at myself as I hung up my jacket and went to the kitchen for a drink and to search for dinner ingredients. Shaking my head in dismay at myself for being scared of an old man out for a stroll before dinner, I poured myself a glass of water from the kitchen sink and drank it down with great thirst. I poured a second glass without looking for anything better and drank it; reassured, I opened the refrigerator to try to decide what to throw together for Dad's and my dinner tonight. With the colder weather surfacing, I thought soup and sandwiches would fulfill our appetites.

After I opened a couple cans of tomato soup, and I buttered four slices of bread for grilled cheese sandwiches, I reluctantly took my Algebra book from my bag and sat with it open on the kitchen table waiting for Dad to come home. At least I could try to study tonight and hope to come out with a passing grade on the test tomorrow. If I didn't study at all, I had no one to blame but myself, and then I know I'd regret not putting forth the effort at minimum. When Dad came in through the squeaky door to the garage, I could tell that he had had a rough day. I looked up from my textbook and pushed my chair away from the table. Work can be cruel punishment or immense reward, he'd say, all in the same day.

I turned the stove on to begin warming the soup and the pan for the sandwiches. "Not a good day, Dad?" I asked with a tentative smile and a kiss on his cheek.

He returned my smile and kiss but didn't answer me. He walked into the hall to hang up his coat and put his laptop bag near the stairs to be carried up later. I heard him swear in a low voice as I stirred the soup and placed the first pieces of cheese on the bread in the pan. He walked back into the kitchen with the mail; envelopes were sticking out in all different directions, and he was organizing them back into a neat, ordered pile by tapping them upright on the kitchen table. He laid them down and then pulled out a chair for himself, sighed, and picked them up again. The table seeped with blue from his sleeves and rose around him. If only there were something I could do to soothe his sadness. He hid it from me though. So we just play the appearances on days like today—most days. Everything is just fine.

I told him about my day, leaving out the panic attack before the after school bus ride, and tried to connect with him on some level about his work day. I hadn't had a chance to play any piano yet tonight, so I asked him if he minded if I played for a little while and then returned to studying for my Algebra test. He thought that was a perfect idea so that he'd have some peaceful music to accompany his cleaning up the kitchen for us after our meal and reading the mail. Then, he said he'd check on my studying and help me with any questions I had before bed. Mom wouldn't have agreed. She would have said I'd be better off getting the studying out of the way; then, I could relax and enjoy playing for as long as I liked. So, thinking of pleasing her, I changed my mind and studied at the table while Dad cleaned up. Then, he sat down with me to read the mail. While tearing open envelopes and making piles of bills, junk mail, and catalogs or stuff to read later, it was actually helpful to have him right there to ask questions.

We must have sat together at the kitchen table for at least a half an hour before we both started to lean back in our chairs and look at each other with a glance that said even though we both don't feel like doing what we're doing, it's nice to have company to make the tasks seem less like punishment. I pushed back my chair from the table after another ten minutes or so accepting the fact that I knew what I was going to know for my Algebra test tomorrow. I stood up and stretched my arms low behind my back with my fingers entwined. Dad nodded at me with a smile with silent permission to go play the piano. I piled up my books on the table and kissed Dad on the cheek leaving him alone to listen to my playing without worrying about whether I could see the emotions it may elicit.

I had always shared this time with Mom not Dad, so it still brings out a mixture of longing for my mother's presence as well as peace and pride in the songs I play. I needed to play tonight. Silver dust rose from the keys as I started to warm up. I closed my eyes to better hear the music's beauty, but I could tell when Dad was standing behind me. My violet lay heavier on my chest; I figured it was turning a deep sea blue from its outer edges towards its violet middle. I felt a healing in my heart, just a start, but it was there. When I finished playing the piece, Dad put his hand on my shoulder and sat down facing away from the piano, his back towards the keys.

"No matter what, you'll always have this gift from your mother." He inhaled and let the air out with a sigh. "It'll have to be enough for us both," he resigned.

"We have each other, Dad. That's enough," I said as I began to play again. "One more before bed."

"It sounds beautiful," he said as he stood up and walked over to a high backed chair on the other side of the room. Instead of sitting down, he stayed facing that chair with his hand resting on its back. I guessed he was looking at the wedding photograph of himself and my mother that hung on the wall behind the chair.

I kept playing. Although I know that Dad was feeling sad, and probably still anger too, I was enjoying playing tonight. My arms were strong; my fingers graceful, and the notes came out fluffy and white. I was taking the right steps to take care of us. It wasn't going to be easy, but we'd make it.

Dad slept restfully that night. I was convinced that my music helped. Even though she wasn't here, I knew Mom would have liked that.

Her letter was on white, raw textured paper that felt heavy like a bouquet:

My Little Violet,
There is time enough in a day to do everything. Do what
you have to do and then what you want to do. It'll make
you feel accomplished and teach you to manage your time.

Chapter 4

TODAY was going to be a busy day. I was drawn to wearing red today—an auburn red sweater that has flecks of brown, beige, and orange in it. Just pulling it over my head made my temperature rise with anxiety over the test I had in Algebra today and our team's last field hockey game. Over my jeans, I tugged on my beige boots that had faux wool on the inside. My bedroom was cool this morning as I dressed. My own heat warmed the space around me from the chill of the night.

I was packing my lunch while eating a bowl of cereal, so that each time I spooned a bite into my mouth, I was dripping milk on the table or the floor because I went from the pantry to the refrigerator to the sink to wash a piece of fruit to pack into my bag.

"You're making a mess!" Dad startled me with the volume of his scolding.

"Oh, Dad, you scared me. I didn't hear you come down."

"You're going to clean that up, aren't you?" he said with more reprimand in his voice than a question.

"Of course I am," I said annoyed with his tone. "What's gotten to you already this morning?"

"Nothing," Dad snapped with his back to me as he finished pouring his cup of coffee. He walked out to get the newspaper and let the door slam, which he usually doesn't do.

"Obviously something…," I mumbled to myself since he wasn't in the kitchen.

Unfortunately I didn't have time to figure out what was frustrating my father this morning, but I had noticed the color of my sweater replicated in the room. I refused the flicker of red that was forming in my mind. I needed to catch the bus shortly and wanted to have a clear head to approach the Algebra test, and I was mad that Dad was starting off my morning by taking focus off of my priorities. I just didn't have the energy to worry about him today—he's an adult and can work it out for himself. I guess he forgot about that peaceful night's sleep he had. I thought I'd made him free of the blues for now. He was positively infused with red today. Maybe my choice of music didn't do the trick.

I shoved my books from the pile I had left on the kitchen table last night into my backpack along with my lunch. Pouring the leftover cereal and milk into the sink that I no longer had the stomach for, I put the bowl and spoon in the dishwasher and grabbed a paper towel to wipe up my drops of milk from their landing spots on the table and the floor. Dad let the door slam again when he came back inside from retrieving today's newspaper. Bent over on the floor, I hadn't expected it and almost literally jumped out of my boots.

"Do you have to let the door slam so early in the morning? You'll wake up the birds with that noise," I said, because I like everything quiet until I wake up fully. In fact I don't typically talk much at all till I get to school. Dad knows that and is usually the same way.

"You're leaving, aren't you? So what's the difference what noise I make?"

I was surprised at the meanness of Dad's answer to me, but I saw the rise in auburn brown and red around him as I put on my coat and picked up my backpack to leave. I tried to listen to his thoughts, but my own irritation with him made it difficult.

"Whatever," I said back with more disappointment in him than belligerence. I was mad at his lack of understanding that I was feeling overwhelmed with the test and the field hockey game today, and I didn't have the patience to try to understand his frustration and why he was being petty and testy with his first words of the day. I zipped up my bag and swung it around my back with an extra urge from my shoulder because of my coat. I left through the door without letting it slam shut but also without saying good-bye to my father. As annoyed as I was, I didn't even feel bad about it.

I walked purposefully towards the bus stop cutting across the yard of the next house to make it to the corner faster as if that would make the bus come more quickly. I didn't even look back at the house to see if Dad was watching me, like I usually do. I kept my back to our house and surged ahead up the stairs of the bus when it arrived a few minutes later. I resisted the impulse to look out the bus window back at the house again and instead searched my bag for my copy of *To Kill A Mockingbird* to both ignore my desire to call my dad and to clear my mind before the Algebra test today.

I opened the novel to the place I last stopped and subconsciously pulled my violet on its cord to my lips to breathe in its spirit, which released the confusion I felt about Dad's treatment of me just now. As much as he's sad without Mom, he's passionately angry as well. I really tried not to envy the relationship that Scout had with her older brother Jem. It must've been comforting to wake up every day knowing that you had someone who would always be there for you, to stand up for you in school, to pretend and play with you in the neighborhood, to dream with you in the dark.

I've often wondered why Mom and Dad didn't have any more children. They seemed to have so much love to give. Dad said this way he had more love to give just to me, which is nice to say, but I don't truly think that is the crux of it. They both gave me all of their attention but never spoiled me with it. I had (still have) chores to do and was always expected to be appreciative of what we had, which wasn't always a lot. I didn't get everything I wanted, not because we couldn't figure out how to afford it, but because it wasn't necessary. When school started in the fall, for instance, I was allowed to get a few new outfits, more because I had outgrown some jeans or my arms were sticking out of sleeves that were too short. Now that my body has decided it has achieved its maximum shape and size in eighth grade, I am still allowed to get a few new things. But I don't take advantage. At Christmastime, when a lot of other kids come back to school with brand new cellphones or trendy sneakers, I may get a small gift on each night of Hanukkah, like a new novel to read or some new perfume. It's no use to wish I had a sibling or even a cousin who lived close to us. I've gotten used to our small family and that's why it's even harder when we disagree or fight. I have no doubt that whatever was bothering Dad this morning, or when something gets my blood boiling, we have no choice but to remind ourselves of the importance of our bond and the fact that we need to remember the strength of the bond. That bond, the one that Dad had with Mom, is probably the very reason he was not himself this morning. He longs to fill up the hole, probably with cement, just like the way Mr. Radley filled the knot-hole in the Scout's tree. Mr. Radley said it was dying, but Scout just knew it was still alive.

I am not always glad to have math first thing in the school day, but the positive part is that I could get that rotten test over with. Austin probably thought I was being a witch because I barely answered his greeting when we arrived at math class. I actually had a boost in my spirit because I felt that my studying had paid off; I think I did pretty well on the test despite the distraction of my dad's attitude I had to ignore. What felt best was to have finished it first thing of the day and to go on feeling slightly accomplished for the rest of the day. I sometimes fight with my own conscience and consider trying to read the teacher's mind, but my gift doesn't seem to work that way. I'd never be able to know what exact questions would be on the test anyway, so what would be the point.

I looked forward to getting to English class. Ms. Stine often let us have a majority of the period to read on Fridays when it fit into her lesson plans, and I figured it would be nice to have a chance to read considering I had been concentrating on studying math, one of my least favorite ways to spend my time. On my path to class in the hallway, I passed Mindy. We moved to the side of the hallway in a little alcove out of the stream of foot traffic, so that others who were talking and walking could pass unobstructed while we stole a minute to catch up with each other.

"Hey, how was the Algebra test?" Mindy asked expectantly. She was also wearing red today. While mine had orange undertones, hers was a truer red, flashy and eye-catching like a siren.

"I think I did okay, so if you studied, I don't think you'll find it too hard," I said.

Mindy nodded with a glimpse of relief. "Okay, yeah, sounds okay." She seemed distracted thinking about it then brightened up. "So, I am so excited for the last game tonight that I almost forgot to bring my uniform with me." She laughed and readjusted her books against her body. Just as I was about to ask Mindy whether she wanted to celebrate after the game, she added, "Well, let me go and get it over with. I'll see you at lunch." Mindy continued on down the hallway in the direction I had just left while I headed the other way.

As I waited a fraction of a second before finding a slot to slide into the flow of people walking on the right side of the hallway, the girl with the Slam Book was strutting by. She seemed to take up more space than she required because of the way she strutted, her elbows jutting into the girls beside her, making them squeeze closer to the wall and the drift of kids walking the other direction.

I noticed that the girls seemed uncomfortable while she seemed not to be bothered by the fact that her friends, if that's what they were, couldn't walk with their own personal space about them.

"You're joking!" she was saying.

I joined the pool of people behind her and kept the pace. The color surrounding her was a dark red, like a glass of burgundy wine, dull and dark and full of self-importance and bitterness. Her essence gave my stomach a twist.

"Who would want to hang out there? I'm not interested in going to see Christmas lights. That's for little kids!" she whisked her nose in the air as she spoke.

"Well, that's where the field hockey team is planning to go after the game. A few of the parents volunteered to drive there after we stop at Friendly's for ice cream," Harley, one of my team-mates, said to the girl with a note of irritation. It made me wonder how close friends they actually were. She noticed me behind them just then. "Hey! Hi, Violet!" she said surprised but with sincerity. "Did you hear that the team is heading to Hershey tonight after our game? To Sweet Lights. Have you ever been there? It's really cool. My parents take me and my sister every year."

Harley slowed her pace so that she could walk next to me. I still was wondering how good a friend she and the girl with the Slam Book were. Harley was one of those glamorous girls who didn't flaunt it or even seem to know it. She is not especially tall; in fact she's a lot shorter than I thought as we walked next to each other. But she is fit and lean with hair the color of espresso, darker and shinier than my dark brown hair. Hers is really cork-screw curly too, and it bounces even when it's in a ponytail because it's so thick. As soon as she stepped next to me, her green color became more apparent to me. A lime lollipop green that reminded me of the green highlighter I like to use in class. Harley always seems balanced to me—doesn't go extreme about anything. She's easy to believe, and I trusted her because she's never given me any reason not to.

"I haven't ever been there. But that sounds like a good idea if I can find a ride." I knew that my dad would come to the field hockey game but would be tired and want to head home after the game, although he'd let me go out and celebrate with the team. I tried to sound genuinely excited about going to Hershey's Sweet Lights, but I subconsciously grabbed the violet around my neck and began to slide it left to right on its cord as my anxiety grew from thinking about doing something I had never done before.

"I'm sure there'll be room with someone. I don't know who's all going, but it'll be fun. Make sure to tell Mindy too," Harley said with a smile. "See ya' then." As she turned into a classroom, with her went the green, balanced feeling.

"Great. See you later." I walked a little faster as the hallway began to diminish in sound and color because the bell was about to ring to signal the start of the next period, and I thought about tonight's activities, trying to psych myself up for the game and everything. I was still holding on to my violet feeling its connection relieve my fears.

I guess my parents never took me to Hershey's Sweet Lights because we didn't make a big deal of Christmas and celebrated Hanukkah, but I've heard that it's quite a spectacular display of holiday lights illuminating a car path. What should I be scared of? It's just riding in a car looking at Christmas lights twinkling. Mindy will probably be with me, and we'll probably be listening to holiday songs on the radio and trying to sing along. I don't know why I had this wave of bubbles rushing inside my stomach just thinking about it.

Having some time to read in English class helped calm my mood and my mind. I found it interesting the lesson that Scout learned about using language correctly and how using certain words make a person sound "common," like the "n" word. I know that a lot of my peers let words gush out of their mouths with no idea what kind of character the language conveys. It's one thing to want to sound cool or mature; it's quite another when it comes out ignorant and condescending. Obviously, in school we can get into trouble for making racial slurs or bullying. The problem is that these statements don't occur in front of a teacher usually, or the words come out of the mouths of bullies to whom not many will stand up. That might be how Slam Books became so interesting. They're secret and slanderous.

While Ms. Stine's class was relatively silent reading the novel, the girl with the Slam Book entered the room stomping her feet with no regard for the fact that she was interrupting us. Walking right up to Ms. Stine at her desk, she held out one of those universal, goldenrod office envelopes at arm's length.

"What's this?" Ms. Stine asked her as she had no choice but to take the envelope inches from her face.

"My parents. They want you to fill these out," she said with a mix of boldness and uncertainty. The girl barely completed her words and turned right around on her heels to leave.

"Well...wait a minute. Alexis, I...I don't understand. What...?" Ms. Stine just looked after the girl, Alexis. Now I knew her name. She was gone as quickly as she had arrived; the vision from her colors wasn't complete, which kind of relieved me. I was a little unnerved at her demeanor with Ms. Stine and was afraid of what I might see.

I couldn't help but watch Ms. Stine open the envelope that Alexis had left with her, even though I wanted to return to my reading that was still intriguing me with its history and characters. Ms. Stine pulled out a short stack of papers and rifled through them for about a minute scanning with no visible display on her face. She squinted her eyes, laid her elbow on her desk and rubbed her forehead with her thumb and forefinger for a couple seconds. She replaced the papers in the envelope and put them on top of the pile of what I presumed was other work to do. Ms. Stine rose from her chair and walked into the hallway. It looked as if she were trying to catch Alexis before she completely disappeared. Ms. Stine turned her head in both directions, like following a tennis match for a couple volleys, and then she came back into the classroom. She glanced up at the clock that was mounted above the door to the classroom.

"You have about ten minutes left to read. You might think about writing in your log so that you have a response or summary or both for today, if you're ready to do that. I hope you enjoyed your time to read today."

About ten minutes later Ms. Stine wished us a good weekend and we left. She kept rubbing her forehead after Alexis had interrupted class, so I couldn't be sure that she'd have the good weekend she just wished us.

At lunch I talked with Mindy about going to Sweet Lights in Hershey with the field hockey team. Of course she had already heard about going and arranged for us to ride with Stacey. I had mixed feelings about the whole trip. I wanted so desperately to enjoy going out with the team and to feel relaxed about it, to anticipate it even. Now the thought of scrunching into Stacey's mom's SUV with a gaggle of girls, who will be excited and over-the-top with the end of the season's accomplishment made my stomach tense. Mindy noticed that I was toying with my violet, and I noticed that her melon color turned a shade of yellow near her heart. She faced me, put her hands on my shoulders and forced me to straighten up.

"Vi. It's gonna be fun. You deserve it. You played a good season, and it's just a bunch of us going out for ice cream and riding around looking at Christmas lights. There's nothing to worry about." She paused to look me in the eye, and I felt her compassion release the tension in my chest and shoulders. A tinge of uncertainty lingered in my stomach.

I nodded. "I know," I said quietly.

"Text your dad while we're getting ready for the game to let him know. Don't forget." She gave my shoulders a friendly shake, and smiled at me with her melon-yellow spark.

I gave an audible exhale as I gathered my books from the cafeteria table knowing that she was right. We spent history class, our last class of the day, thinking mostly about the game and harnessing our energies till then. I sent Dad a text from the locker room, not sure whether he was even planning on coming to the last game. I had mostly forgotten about our tiff this morning, as I tend to do. I didn't have time to wait around for Dad's response about whether he'd allow me to go to Hershey with the girls, but I figured I'd either see him at the game or receive a text from him by the time the game ended.

As usual I didn't start the game, as Mindy does. By the end though, I had played about 7 minutes or so in each half. It was nice to win the game even though we scored the one and only goal. It was Harley. Quick and strong down the field. I envy her confidence. Mom says that envy breeds nothing but more jealousy. Yeah, but what else am I supposed to feel when I admire someone's skills I'll never have?

While sitting on the bench with my teammates, I quietly hummed a tune that Mom and I played on the piano sometimes. "Evergreen," I think it's called. I don't know the words, just the notes. I know no one could hear me. I guess I was probably being unsocial by not cheering the team on, but I don't think anyone noticed. Harley was so fast down the field—her legs were like wheels accelerating before she scored. I started to listen to Harley's thoughts to use them to improve my game, but the song kept coming back into my head. Finding solace in the song I heard in my head, I let my memory drift away for a few moments. I watched the game in front of me but didn't really see it.

I wanted more from this letter from Mom. The words didn't fit the fancy script she used on sky blue paper sprinkled with tiny daisies, white and yellow:

My Little Violet,
Take a deep breath. It simply makes your head clear. I think it's the oxygen.

Chapter 5

O H, for the love of chocolate. Dad had been able to come to watch the field hockey game since he had spent his Friday working from home. He had replied to my text message before the start of the game, but I hadn't had a chance to see it. He said that it was fine if I went out with the team after the game and that he was on his way to watch. Dad is incredibly supportive of anything I do, and I was glad, actually proud, that he was sitting in the bleachers in his winter jacket and gloves drinking from a paper cup from the coffee kiosk at the grocery store. I noticed him from my seat on the bench with the other girls that didn't start the game. He raised his cup to me in a toast, which was also his peace offering since his fight with me this morning. I discounted his anger because I didn't really think it was directed at me; even though it's not fair to take out his missing Mom on me, I was mature enough to understand that he couldn't hold it inside all the time. The fact that Dad and I could sweep away the brief periods of increased annoyance with each other restored our relationship better than before. I think I understand better than most eighth graders how relationships require a give-and-take each day; no one is perfect, but if you love someone, you have to expect to have to travel through the darkest of nights sometimes to reach the brightest of days and appreciate them. Dad looked fresher to me. His typical arctic blue was breezy with green after the game. I didn't know how his spirit had healed so from the red lightning of this morning, but I was glad it had.

Holding my stick with my hands under my chin, I had waved at him with an obscure spread of the fingers next to my face and then reached for my violet around my neck out of habit, forgetting that during field hockey games was the only time that I took off my necklace because we aren't allowed to wear any jewelry when playing. I kept my eyes locked with Dad's as I realized it was more than my neck that felt empty. Without my violet, there felt like there was little oxygen, no strength in my body. I knew it was only a necklace, but it felt like more than that—I only miss it when it's gone.

I took a deep breath, grasped my stick with both hands and rested my lips against my fingers. I blinked my eyes slowly letting the blackness behind my lids separate me from the intensity of the game in front of me. I let the "Evergreen" song keep going in my head, imagining I was playing the actual keys on the piano at home. When I opened my eyes to see the cobalt blue of our uniforms and the green surrounding Dad beside the game, I released my breath not realizing I was holding it that whole time. I'm sure I wasn't focused on much of the game, but Harley's green streaked out behind her as we all crowded around to congratulate each other on the win.

Dad met me on my walk back to the locker room with the team. He said, "Good game, ladies." He was met with a round of responsive "thank you's" from a number of the girls who appreciated his words. He patted me on the back and squeezed my shoulder in approval.

"Thanks for coming, Dad."

"You know I wouldn't miss your last game." Those words were infused with an apologetic tone. He bent his head near mine and lowered his voice with softness. He was quiet for a moment and then told me to go have fun this evening with the girls and to call if I needed him for a ride or anything else. I had a notion he felt a mixture of uncertainty and encouragement behind his words, almost exactly how I felt about going myself.

Stacey gathered a group of girls from the locker room in the haze of our victorious game and packed us into her mom's SUV. Stacey herself wanted to be in the third row seat, so she was actually one of the first ones into the car. I sat behind Stacey's mom, and Mindy sat next to me. There were three other girls in the very back with Stacey, and Harley was sitting on the other side of Mindy. One of our assistant coaches plopped into the front seat next to Stacey's mom. She passed around coupons for free ice cream sundaes at Friendly's.

"Awesome way to end the season, ladies," the coach said with her booming voice, better suited to the field than an enclosed space. I winced. I think she realized her volume when she began again, still looking back at all of us in our seats, "I am so proud of all of you. Let's go see some Sweet Lights!"

We held onto our ice cream coupons as our chatter rose and fell during the fifteen minutes it took to arrive at Friendly's. We met up with the other few vehicles also carting our team through our celebration for the evening. In the parking lot we really started getting loud and the number in our crowd seemed to me to grow instantaneously. The night air wasn't cold enough to see my breath, but I felt the warmth of the others close around me. I held onto my violet for calmness, as if to ward off the deepening of the purple petals. I vowed not to ruin this night for myself with my silly fears. I knew we would be walking inside and spreading out at tables to enjoy our ice cream treats, and then we'd be back in the cars again, in small, sensible groups. I had control. I kept telling myself that I had control. I looked up at the lights mounted on the edges of the restaurant's roof, like silver cones of rose-colored light, and a split second presence of my mother appeared to me and then vanished. I wasn't sure I saw anything at all, but I sensed her above like a halo. I wondered whether she was trying to help me relax and enjoy tonight, or whether I was imagining it all and in complete absence of my sanity.

"Did you see that?" Mindy asked me.

"What?!" I asked with incredulity. Did she see something too?

"Austin is here," Mindy said as quietly as she could restrain her enthusiasm. She was almost skipping through the door of Friendly's, pushing me ahead of her as if to shield her emotions from knocking him over.

I had no choice but to let my mind drift back to the present and join the party. I had my coupon in one hand and my violet in the other and a tiny furrow forming between my brows as I wondered what just happened outside in the darkness.

Apparently, a group of eighth-graders had decided to join the field hockey team this Friday night to honor our last game. I think it was just the place to be on a Friday night if you weren't at one of the local high school football games, which would be the cause for the crowd that showed up a little later. Austin was seated at a table with mostly boys from the baseball team. The football season would be coming to an end soon, so I guess he was gearing up for spring baseball training sessions. I knew Mindy would be searching for Brittany, just to make sure he hadn't gone back on his word and rekindled their coupledom. My mind wasn't quite connected with Mindy's love life just yet; I was still lingering on that rose-colored light.

There were tables pushed together for us near the back of the place, so we had to walk right by Austin and his buddies in a booth.

Because Mindy was pushing me first, I had to say hello first, which I did. I couldn't tell whether Austin actually said hi, because all the girls behind us were creating an increasing wave of conversation as we moved towards the tables reserved for our team. I would bet that Mindy didn't say a word and just smiled her melon-charged smile. Thinking of that eased the line in my forehead, and I patted the pendant around my neck one last time before pulling out a chair and sitting down with satisfaction at having survived the crowd outside without being overcome with panic.

I was having a great time in fact. We gave our orders for various sundaes to the several servers assigned to us. We were reliving highlights from this last game as well as other plays that were memorable. Ice cream spoons were dripping chocolate sauce and melted flavors on the paper placemats, unwanted cherries were being passed by the stems to cherry-lovers, bottoms of dishes were scraped while others sat filling up with lumps of whipped cream layered on top of melted ice cream. If I had to choose a favorite ice cream, I don't think that I could. I go for whatever flavor strikes my mood. But tonight I ordered a Reese's Pieces sundae—vanilla swirled with chocolate and peanut butter syrups and sprinkled with peanut butter candies coated in chocolate shells on top of the puff of whipped cream. I couldn't finish the whole thing, but I tried. By the time I got near to my fill, most of the girls were also getting ready to leave and continue down the road to Hershey's Sweet Lights. The servers were filling up a few more water glasses and collecting our coupons as we would soon be leaving. Then I heard her.

A voice was coming from a video being played back on some-one's phone. "…I expected this to be taken care of already…waited till now…I know what the problem is here, isn't it…JUST MAKE SURE OF IT!"

Alexis closed her phone and said, "If anything, Ms. Stine's going to quit. She can't just get away with that…." Her comments were met with a table full of agreement, although I didn't recognize all of the girls sitting around Alexis.

I wasn't sure if I heard her right. Ms. Stine? Were they all really talking about Ms. Stine quitting? I can't believe that anyone would think that Ms. Stine would be anything but real and helpful. I probably would put her up there as one of the best teachers I ever had. Yeah, she wasn't perfect and she got annoyed with things, but what teacher doesn't? With only Alexis' vicious scarlet wafting in the air, I had little to go on. Alexis, her phone, Ms. Stine, the cafeteria. It seemed like the game of Clue, and it was time to go.

We left our table bouncing like bubbles in the air. I really noticed that I needed my winter jacket. The temperature had really begun to drop for an early December evening. We exited the parking lot in an uninterrupted tide down the road to find the entrance to Hershey's Sweet Lights. We actually could see glimpses of twinkling lights behind the black skeletons that were leafless trees. The traffic slowed to approach the entrance. The sugar from the ice cream sundae and the anticipation of seeing something new for the first time warmed my body to the point that I almost wanted to take off my jacket. Mindy was chattering nonstop next to me, and Stacey was rattling off a list of some of her most favorite lights to see. We were all in the holiday spirit.

We arrived to Sweet Lights, and I was stunned. The colors. All the amazing colors. How could I have never seen this before? It was as if the illumination made sense to me. I had a crystal clear feeling inside for the first time I can recall. Complete understanding calmed my heart; no worries were lurching in my belly or tying knots in my breaths. The myriad white lights energized me, glistening from each tiny light. Down the path we went: elves appearing in green and red, reindeer teams guiding a sleigh, Santa waving to us in his usual attire. We all waved back giggling and embarrassed, like children seeing the real Santa for the first time. Angels floated with golden wings and rose-colored hair. Rose. I'm not sure how I knew it, but I did. These were the colors of my mom. I squinted and leaned up against the cold glass of the car window, my breath making a circle of moisture immediately. I had to lean back so that I could see clearly. What I saw didn't make me panic like I thought it would. It gave me an idea. Actually, I wondered why I hadn't thought of it before.

The ride home to Dad gave me peace. I had enjoyed seeing all of the formations of light sprouting from the forest along the wooded path and singing along to Christmas carols with the radio and the carload of girls who were becoming part of this milestone for me. The field hockey season was over, and I was still debating whether to pursue it as a freshman in high school next fall. But I had time to decide. For now I took a moment to be proud of myself for completing the season and letting myself have some fun. Even though I wished for my mother to be able to share it with me, I felt like she was there in some way. I had made some new friends and understood that that was what Mom would have wanted, to keep going, even in baby steps. I think I was beginning to understand myself a little bit more today. I had a sense of accomplishment, and I haven't appreciated that very often in my life, but it felt good.

I had snapped a few photos with my phone from Sweet Lights and sent one to Dad with the message, "home soon," so that he'd know to expect me. Stacey had asked if all the girls had wanted to sleep over, but I had enough for the day. If it had just been Mindy, or maybe even Harley too, I may have reconsidered. But I didn't feel like it. I was tired, and I was thinking about Mom and Dad. I don't think family means as much to people who have a solid one and never know what it's like to be without—like not knowing what you're missing. But it's different when you do know what you're missing. It hurts. And sometimes not even pretty lights, sweet ice cream, and good friends can fix it.

When I was dropped off at home, I thanked Stacey's mom and the coach and said good-bye to all the girls. They were all going to go back to Stacey's for what I figured was going to be a long night of watching movies, eating more junk food, and probably texting boys. That would've entailed some mind-reading I didn't have the energy for tonight. I ran up to the front door since Dad had left the lights on for me. I tried to close the door quietly and take my shoes and coat off in the foyer before going straight up the stairs to bed. Dad came out of the dark kitchen while my back was turned. Hanging up my coat and kicking my shoes off into the closet, he startled me. He had a bowl of cereal in his palm and spoke to me with a mouthful.

"How was your evening?" he asked.

"Oh, Dad," I said with a jump, my back leaned up against the front door. "I thought you were asleep." My surprise turned into a relieved but tired smile. "Great. Fun. I'm really glad I went. We should go sometime. You and me." The thought of the rose-colored angel leaped into my head, and I wrapped my thumb and fingers around my neck where my violet hung.

"Hmm...ok," he mumbled, and he walked over to kiss me on the forehead. The milk from his kiss seemed to linger, so I wiped it off with the back of my hand. I narrowed my eyes in the darkness of the foyer, because the wetness looked rose-colored. I rubbed it off on my jeans and looked at the back of my hand again. It wasn't there.

I looked up at Dad's face. He smiled and turned to take his bowl back into the kitchen. I started up the stairs to bed under the faint light of the nightlight coming from the bathroom at the top of the stairs, and I heard him lay the bowl and spoon with a clink into the sink. I didn't turn on the light in my bathroom when I went in to brush my teeth but looked at myself in the mirror and thought I saw the imprint of Dad's kiss on my forehead in the shadows. I flipped up the switch. It wasn't there. I must be tired. I brushed my teeth, went to my bedroom and changed into a t-shirt to sleep in, and I got into bed. I plugged in my phone to charge on my nightstand. Just as I was about to get back out of bed to turn off my overhead light, Dad poked his head in.

"Do you want your light off?" he asked.

"Yes, thanks. I'm more tired than I thought," I answered as I pushed all the decorative pillows off my bed, scooted down under the covers and lay my head on the pillow. "Good night. Oh, and thanks."

"For coming to your game? Or for letting you go to Hershey?"

"Just thanks. For being my dad." I closed my eyes with a smile. Dad had turned off the light before I could see what sort of reaction he returned. I looked, but my eyes hadn't yet adjusted to the darkness. My phone reflected on the frame with my mother's picture in it, and for a second the glow looked rosy instead of angel-white. It played its short declining scale as I shut it off for the night. I knew the color couldn't have been real. But it reminded me of that idea I had. And with that, I fell asleep.

Mom's note was on paper the color of red roses. It had a sheen to it that faded and darkened depending upon the light.

My Little Violet,
Eat chocolate-covered strawberries. They are divine. Treat yourself at least once a day. Do the same for someone else.

Chapter 6

Ihad no idea what time it was when I opened my eyes Saturday morning. I was rested and hungry, so I didn't think it was anywhere near the time I was used to getting up for school. Although I didn't say it aloud, I said "good morning" to my mother in her picture when I picked up my phone from the nightstand to see what time it was. Just after ten. I'm sure Dad had already eaten and was reading or working by now. I made my bed as soon as I got out of it. I do that almost every day, even weekends. I just like how soft and inviting my room looks when all the pastel pillows are piled high on my bed and everything looks neat. I hopped down the stairs calling for Dad.

I walked into the kitchen expecting him to be drinking coffee in there. When I hadn't run into him yet, I saw a note on the table. "Went to temple. Back before lunch." That was unusual. I started searching the refrigerator for tempting breakfast foods and wondered why he had decided to go to synagogue this morning. When I was younger, I went to Hebrew school once a week and on Sundays to prepare for my Bat Mitzvah. I remember really feeling grown up before symbolically becoming an adult. It's funny how I feel less grown up now that I know more. We started attending services on Fridays and Saturdays more frequently to celebrate the Jewish Sabbath. Dad never minded going, but I didn't think that he was doing it for more than just an obligation to me and my education. He and my mother were both raised Jewish, but her father wasn't Jewish. My grandfather always brought me chocolate ducks at Easter and sat me on his lap to sing me songs at Christmastime. I've never met either of my grandmothers though; they were gone before I was born. My father's father, Poppop, is still living in a home for the elderly about a half hour from here. We make visits to him when we can, not necessarily on any special occasion. We'll probably go over my Winter Break from school. He's the storyteller of the family.

One of my favorite stories that Poppop told me is about a time he was eating lunch at a drug store counter in Woolworth's in New York City shortly after he came to America from Germany in the late 1930s. A snack bar, diner-type set up is how he described the counter in the drug store. He couldn't speak much English then, but he had a job in a factory, so it didn't much matter yet. He was beginning to learn about American customs, and when it came to food, it was easy to simply get a bowl of pea soup with bread for dipping, costing only pennies here. One day, he told me, he was having lunch on a particularly hot day with a gentleman whom my grandfather was trying to impress. I think he was looking to move up as a salesman in the company or something like that. The other man had ordered a milkshake to drink, so my grandfather just ordered the same thing. When the server placed the tall glass filled with the thick creamy drink in front of him, my grandfather didn't know how to begin. With a spoon? Sip it? He dramatically described how parched his throat was, yet he didn't want to offend the man by doing anything inappropriately and looking like a fool. So he sat there and waited and waited till the other man finally poked a long straw into the beveled glass and drew in the liquid, ultimately showing my grandfather what to do. How he longed to quench his thirst that day! I'll never know how my grandfather felt as a foreigner, yet I know how it feels to be afraid of making a mistake.

So, I guess Dad felt he needed some guidance, some prayers, some time and space to reflect on life. As I dug out some frozen multigrain waffles from the freezer and laid them in the toaster oven, I felt some misgivings about not having woken up to join him. I'm sure Dad wanted to let me sleep off my busy week, but I would have happily gone with him just to keep him company and help him have another good day instead of a bad one.

I poured blueberry syrup on my waffle and a small glass of milk and sat at the table by myself, beginning already to grow impatient with the quiet and not having anyone to talk to or anything planned to do today. I half-realized this because I was tapping the top of my foot against the table leg harder and harder until I almost knocked over my glass of milk. I shoved the last few bites of my breakfast down and knew I had at least an hour before Dad would return, if not two. So, I put my dishes in the dishwasher and went upstairs to get dressed. Deciding what to do with myself, I looked out my bedroom window to see what the weather for the day looked like so far. It looked mostly sunny, gray shadows from the aging trees danced on the sidewalk, but I could feel a chill air prickle my arms while standing close to the window, so I wasn't deceived that it was to be an unseasonably warm day in December. I couldn't see Mrs. Suden's house from my vantage point, but I could see the sale sign in the grass by the street, which was the signal for what to do with my free time.

I picked out a pair of clean but worn jeans, a camisole and t-shirt both in shades of lavender. I slid on my boots that have the soft fur inside that feel so warm even without socks. After brushing my teeth, I smoothed my hair back into a knot with an elastic band, and had just stepped into the hallway, when I decided to go back into my room and put on my Cobalt Valley sweatshirt instead of wearing my winter coat. I was only going next door after all. I put my phone and house key in the center pocket of my sweatshirt and shut the front door behind me, replacing my hands inside the pocket to keep them warm.

I walked with more purpose than necessary towards the house, as I really was just visiting out of curiosity and leisure. I looked up at the blue sky. It was one of those clear days that had not a cloud to be seen, and the blue looked like the sea on a map in the geography book, flat and endless. I noticed three balloons that were tied to the street sign post, one white and the other two matched the patriotic red of the real estate agent's sign stuck in the yard. It didn't look like a party when I approached the front porch though. Not a person to be seen. I knocked faintly and turned the knob to easily open the door to my neighbor's house. I felt obtrusive, like I was doing something I should feel guilty for; I even looked side to side before stepping inside as if someone would catch me committing unlawful entry or some such crime.

Immediately, I was overcome by the scent of cookies baking and a "hello" beckoned with a question mark yet a friendly welcome. I didn't recognize the voice, however. Maybe it was the realtor or Mrs. Suden's son. For a split second I was surprised that I wasn't panicking by doing something as brave as exploring an unknown house, but I was reminded why there was complete calm in my belly and no worry in my chest. Mrs. Suden had let me play in her yard when I was a little girl, and so I felt comfortable here. She'd give me chocolates or lemonade once in a while when she'd see me outside playing by myself. The colors in her foyer surrounded me, pale yellows and greens, child-like colors and simple feelings with no hidden secrets behind them.

"Hello," I called in a voice much louder than I usually use, but friendly, polite. "It's your neighbor, Violet."

A guy much younger than I expected came out from the kitchen with a half-eaten cookie in his left hand. He extended his right hand to me in greeting.

"Hey, I'm Breck. My father is selling this house. You live next door?" he asked.

I wasn't sure how much information to give him, but I had already said as much. "Yeah, um, yes. My father and I do." I was studying his face and didn't want to give away that I was mesmerized by his colors. "Violet," I said. "I mean, I'm Violet."

I hadn't ever met anyone who exuded a stream of violet so similar to mine, to the one around my neck. I was mystified and probably came off like an airhead.

"Nice to meet you, Violet." He turned back towards the kitchen. "Want a cookie? I just baked them," he offered, and then he raised his shoulders and placed the back of his hand next to his mouth as if to quiet his voice. "Don't tell anyone, but they help appeal to the senses when buyers enter a house. It's supposed to make them feel at home. That's what my dad says."

"No, thank you. I actually just ate breakfast," I said, even though they smelled very enticing. I followed him back into the kitchen. It was a little smaller than ours but similar in layout and clearly had the original workmanship replaced. I tried not to look obvious mentally noting things I liked and didn't, but I like to pretend what I'd change if the house were mine. Like playing house, I guess. The cabinetry was a light sandalwood, and the appliances were black. It looked very clean and classy. The countertops were a stunning black granite with different shades of brown scratched through it. A tall vase of fresh flowers in deep reds and blues sat on the counter.

"Oh, okay." He shrugged his shoulders and helped himself to another cookie. This time he put his index finger across his lips, so as to tell me I should keep his cookie theft a secret. He seemed likable, but I wasn't sure if he was going to let me tour the house without tagging along, especially since there wasn't anyone else there. And, I really wanted to take my time. I had nothing better to do than let my imagination run away through the rooms. I just sort of stood there with my hands in my sweatshirt pocket and tried to peer into the other rooms from the kitchen.

"Look around, Violet. You don't have to stay in here and keep me company," he chuckled, seemingly aware of my intentions. "Go ahead. My dad will be here soon if you have any questions. Although my guess is you're just curious, not serious," he paused and smiled at me. "About buying the house," he added.

"Right," I smiled back, relieved that he was going to let me look around and not follow me around either. "Thanks." And, I hoped I sounded like I meant it as much as I did.

I thought I'd be more comfortable heading right upstairs, so that I could remove my mind from meeting Breck and explore alone for a while. The second floor was also similar in layout to ours, just as I had expected. There was a lot more furniture still in the rooms than I had thought. I guess those home improvement and sales advice shows on TV encourage sellers to make quintessential scenes out of each room, to depersonalize by removing photographs and such, but to beautify and make the most of the selling points. I spent some time sitting on a small, fabric-covered bench that sat underneath the window in what would be my room in my house. I never much looked at my room from this spot, as I'm usually standing and looking at the view out the window, not in. I sat with my back against the wall and stared at the bed and at the nightstand. I liked this bedroom suite because it looked new; mine must've belonged to one of my grandmothers before it was Mom's. But I liked my room, my own space where I could sleep in peace and quiet, store my own memories, yearbooks and photos, ticket stubs and the few awards I'd won. The thing was I didn't have much of that stuff to save. Some but not much. I've just never stood out in any special way nor have I done much of anything exceptional. It's okay, Dad says, because I have time, time for endless dreams and goals to strive for, and any accomplishment is one to be proud of. He's so good at finding the goodness. I've accepted my mediocrity. It's part of who I am. For now.

I slid my hands across the fabric of the bench. I really liked its rounded edges and that it was barely big enough for two to sit. It looked just like a gymnast doing a backbend, her little body flexible enough to make a half circle above the floor. I stood up and was about to walk out without looking in the closet, but I changed my mind. I wondered for a moment what it would be like to open up my closet at home that looked just like this one, and gasp at a brand new wardrobe. Expensive designer jeans and coats. Tops and sweaters in deep hues and supermodel styles. Shoes. Lots of them. I opened the closet door by sliding it. The same as mine, only one door at a time can be opened. It was empty. I was sort of disappointed, just for pretend's sake. I stuck my head in and couldn't see much for it was pretty dark behind the door, so I slid the doors the other way, trying not to make too much noise. I didn't want anyone to think I was being nosy. As expected, nothing on this side either except a plastic rectangle; it looked like an oversized light switch to the right of the door on the inside of the front closet wall, rather narrow, not more than five or six inches. It was missing most of the eight screws it appeared it needed to hold itself in place, but I was unable to move it from its resting spot. I didn't feel as if it was my place to start damaging walls and digging around, but I began to wonder if there was such a spot in my closet, and that intrigued me enough to move my quest along more quickly through the rest of the house.

The other places of interest in the house for me were the master bedroom and the living room, which in our house is the parlor. Mrs. Suden's master bedroom was a palace compared to the "mish mash" of furniture and lackluster style of the pieces in my parents' room. They never bought their own bedroom set and just used a combination of pieces from their pasts. They said that they liked having mementos and inheriting a chair here and a lamp there; it was an eclectic look. Yeah, I guess. They just didn't care about appearances, and who else was going to see their bedroom except them. This master suite had a king-sized bed, its headboard covered in taupe velvet so that it matched the mushroom colors of the wood, which reminded me of the outside of the house. The bath had a make-up vanity where I imagined Mrs. Suden rubbed in her wrinkle creams and teased up her hair do. My mother would have loved a bathroom like this; I am sure she would have let me play dress up, spray on perfume and paint my fingernails. Their bathroom has double sinks and a large stall shower, so it was more than some, but nothing extra fancy. I stood for a moment there in the bathroom and gave my violet a kiss by kissing my fingers and touching the pendant as a wish for my mother. Wherever she was, I hoped she had something extra, something fancy.

After perusing the upstairs, I went downstairs to peek briefly in the dining room and to check out the living room. Even though Mrs. Suden's living room looked posh and pretty with its fluffy cushioned chairs, glass coffee table, and a breakfront presenting an ornate polished silver tea set, I was proud of the unassuming parlor that my mother fashioned with the old upright piano and scalloped chair that sat beside it for anyone who cared to listen to the music. I guess I was in the living room for a while, because Breck's father had popped in to remind me to "take my time," and Breck stood by the archway to the foyer for a minute until he decided to speak to me.

"You seem fascinated by interior decorating. Either that or you *do* want to buy this house," Breck said half-jokingly.

I let out a small laugh. He had broken my reverie, but it was probably time to go home anyway. Dad would be home soon. And, I didn't want to forget to check my own closet for the switch plate. Maybe I could finally have some light in my closet. "I just like walking through houses. This one is almost exactly like mine anyway." I figured I didn't know him well enough to let him in on too many of my thoughts, so I stopped with that.

"I like walking through houses too," Breck offered. "I don't know if it's 'cause my dad has dragged me around for years through sale after sale, or if it's something else." He seemed thoughtful for a moment. "I don't know. It's cool though to imagine yourself living in different places," he affirmed.

I'm sure my eyes registered surprise as I nodded my head. "Definitely cool. Well, I ought to get back home. Nice to meet you."

"You too, Violet. If you see me hanging out here with my dad till he sells the place, feel free to come back over. You know, if you have time," he seemed like he was trying to make an effort to be friends, and I didn't see anything wrong with that. His violet essence didn't give away much. I still wondered how old he was and where he went to school but didn't have the nerve to get into a personal conversation. He seemed like he was willing to get to know me. I started my way out thinking about him.

"Okay, thanks. See ya'," I said without sounding too eager but appreciative just the same. I gave a quick wave behind me as I left out the front door and bounded down the porch steps and over to our yard in a flash. It had gotten noticeably warmer outside, as it was probably approaching noon. I pulled my phone out of my pocket and pressed the key to illuminate the display. I had spent over an hour next door.

I went right upstairs to my bedroom to look for the light switch plate in my closet and was just taking off my boots and sweatshirt when I heard Dad come in through the squeaky door to the garage. I wondered whether that was something that Breck could fix. Being around homes to be sold all the time could make a person quite handy I would assume.

"Vi, I'm home," Dad called.

"Be right down, Dad." I kicked off my boots into the closet

and threw my sweatshirt over my chair and reminded myself that I'd come back up after lunch with Dad. We didn't have anything going on today anyway.

Dad had brought home a pizza for lunch from Pierro's Pizza, our favorite Italian restaurant not far from our house. His half was plain; my half had green peppers and onions. He told me about the Rabbi's sermon and who he saw at the service this morning. I told him about going to see Mrs. Suden's house next door. I didn't mention Breck, for no particular reason other than it seemed unimportant.

"With Hanukkah beginning," Dad recalled, "the Rabbi was talking about the miracles we ignore in our everyday lives. And how important it is not to minimize these things for which we should be grateful. Of course it made me think of your mother," Dad paused and sighed, "but I needed to go and *cleanse my soul*." This last phrase he said with sarcasm, not seriousness, although I knew he meant it seriously underneath it all. He needed a place to release his feelings, whether they were misery, loss or rejuvenation. When I had that idea while at Hershey's Sweet Lights, I knew I had to do something nice for Dad this Hanukkah, with Mom not here.

We finished a good portion of the pizza, and I put the box with the leftovers in the fridge for another time. Dad said he wanted to watch some college football on TV and do some work, so I told him I'd be in my room reading and cleaning up my field hockey equipment since the season was over. So, I went right up to my closet where I needed to find space for that stuff anyway.

Without looking hard, I found the very same light switch in the very same spot on the right inside front wall of my closet. All eight screws were in place. I had to go get a flashlight and screwdriver from the garage. I don't know why I was worried that Dad would get suspicious, but I was. So, I waited a little while and sorted through my field hockey bag. I put dirty clothes and towels in the hamper and cleaned my stick with some furniture polish and one of the dirty towels. I set the stick in my closet and decided that I needed to shake out my bag outside since there was undetermined debris in it. I went to the garage with my bag, shook it out well, and returned to my room with a flashlight and screwdriver and my field hockey bag folded up for storage till summer camp or fall practice, if I went that route.

I unscrewed the switch plate screw by screw. I had to loosen all eight because it wouldn't budge until then. I removed the rectangle from the wall and was speechless when I saw what lay in the small hole in the wall in my closet. I wondered how many years it survived there.

I opened the old thick book that sat in its hiding spot. Inside the leather cover was pressed a perfect rose surrounded by tiny dried violets tied with a gold-trimmed ribbon I recognized from the flower shop at the mall. I was careful with the pages, cracked and parched like a treasure map. It occurred to me that that might be exactly what this was.

My first hope was that this would help me find out where Mom is or why Mom isn't here. But then I looked inside.

This paper felt like downy duck feathers, white and soft and plain.

My Little Violet,
Keep fresh flowers in the kitchen to brighten your mood.
Food and flowers appeal to the same senses and give you
energy.

Chapter 7

I was proud of myself for a change. I got my Algebra test grade back, and I was very pleased with my 88%, just shy of the A I always strive for but never seem to be able to reach in math. I had spent time studying ahead instead of waiting till the last minute and that seemed to pay off. With English class, that was never hard to do. For instance, Sunday was dedicated to reading ahead in *To Kill A Mockingbird* while Dad read the paper and watched football. I liked studying the literature and writing so it never felt as much as a chore as trying to crack puzzles and figuring out problems and reviewing the math concepts. Even so, starting off first period on a Monday with the sweet fruits of my efforts was not only gratifying but encouraging. Maybe I had more skills than I give myself credit for.

I shared my pride in my grade with Austin, who, effortlessly, at least that's how it appeared from my desk, earned his 97%, pretty typical grade range for him. He seemed genuinely proud of me though and gave me a friendly "way to go" and a pat on the back. It was a golden day so far.

In English class we found out that we'd be working in groups as teams of lawyers representing a client who may or may not be innocent of a crime. We'd be responsible for composing our positions and how we should go about representing our case. From our reading of *To Kill A Mockingbird*, I imagined that our client was black in a white town and would be the victim of discrimination, just like in the plot of the book. The whole point was to incorporate the setting of the novel to help us decide whether it was important if our client was the same on the outside as everyone else in the town, just different on the inside. Where no one could see it. Was he honest or lying? Is it truth or perjury?

Ms. Stine chose randomly who would take on the different roles. A group of students who weren't lawyers would be the jury of twelve deciding the fate of the client. I wasn't sure which I'd rather be, lawyer or juror. I couldn't decide which would be more difficult to play out realistically. I didn't care how much work it would take. I mean, reading the book wasn't hard, and I liked it so far anyway. It really made me wonder what it would've been like to live in that period where treating people differently on color was expected, proper even. And how it must've felt to not know fairness and equality in school or to get a job. It's so hard to believe that it wasn't so very long ago either. It was during my parents' lifetime certainly. What's even harder to believe is that not everyone stuck up for one another. People kept to themselves, their own kind. Not many crossed the color lines or were willing to do the hard work necessary, except people like Atticus Finch, Scout and Jem's father in the novel. A white lawyer willing to represent a black man. That probably didn't happen often in the 60s. He taught them more about standing up for others than some people do today. How hard it must have been to have been that upstanding at that time because it's still hard today. To speak out for one another without feeling scared or worried about retribution, attacked by your own, disapproval from small minds but not knowing any better. It made me want to be strong. I felt like there was a tiny bit of courage inside my heart that I had never tended to before, like watering my violet with sunshine and love would brighten it and give me that strength.

I really took to this project, and Ms. Stine informed us that

Austin would be on my team of lawyers, which was going to be interesting. Mindy would be jealous, just a little. I took the packet of instructions and worksheets for planning, stuck it inside my notebook with the copy of my novel, and left class uplifted. I think I actually walked with my nose and shoulders a little higher than normal. I smiled with a sense of purpose. I wondered if lawyers who know they have a battle in store feel the same way.

By the time lunch rolled around, it had been a pretty productive day. Time had flown by fairly quickly with all the busy-ness of a Monday in December. Some of us were recollecting our trip to Friendly's and Hershey's Sweet Lights, passing around photos that had been taken with phones or emailed and printed over the weekend. We weren't permitted to pass around our actual phones during lunch, of course, even though that would have been the easiest way for us to share each other's pictures from Friday evening. All the same, as photos passed through my hands, there was the one in particular of the angel that was special, her lights like a birthday cake in the dark, only the burning tops of the candles illuminated. I could feel the intensity from the picture run through the nerves of my fingertips.

Clay had an interesting story of his weekend to tell. Apparently someone played a trick on him, and what made it so interesting is that he is usually the trickster. His pranks are harmless and all in good natured fun, and I have to admit that he has quite a clever mind. It's actually a shame that Mindy doesn't like him with as much heart as he likes her, because I think he's a quality friend to have.

As he was telling this story, at first I wasn't sure whether I should take him seriously or not, because he is known to tell them for the pure fiction of them and to see who believes the most. In fact his storytelling is so engaging that Ms. Stine, on her lunch duty, crossed her arms and planted her feet in a spot within earshot so that she could hear his intriguing tale.

He started off with the cryptic text message he had received. It was an unknown number, but it appeared to have been sent to a group, so he figured it was plausible. It said:

CV Cavaliers—8th grade party after game

The message gave an address that was near Clay's house, not too far from my neighborhood. Clay said that he and a few others went to the house Saturday after the football game, in the mid-afternoon. Our school's football field doesn't have lights so our home football games are played Saturdays. There was definitely a party going on at the address they found, cars lined up on both sides of the street. When they knocked on the door, a young woman answered. Clay blushed a little when he said so, so I guessed she was pretty.

As Clay was talking, I felt as if I had heard this story before even though I knew I hadn't. I started laughing and then stopped myself till he finished. It's not like I knew exactly what he was going to say, but I had a knowing feeling. I kept listening. When I find myself questioning how I am able to see the colors surrounding each of us, it's all I've ever known, so I've gotten used to it. Then I remember how Dad said it was sometimes best to keep it all to myself. I thought that Mom could give me answers to help me know when I should listen to my thoughts and when to ignore them, and I guess that's why I feel like I pushed her away. It's the way I've always been, and my parents never insisted that I keep it a secret, but I must have learned as the years went by. I eventually knew when to stop mentioning it. No one else could see the colors I saw, so it made more sense for me to keep it to myself. Except for when I feel trapped and overwhelmed by too many people and too many colors, it isn't hard for me to keep what I see inside.

Clay said that the young woman looked at him strangely and said that he must've been mistaken. She had opened the door a little wider so that Clay and the others could see into the living room where a number of women of all ages were seated both on furniture and the carpeted floor. Some held babies on their shoulders or had them cradled in seats on the floor next to brightly colored gift bags and boxes; some women were quite a bit older drinking from china tea cups, and one obviously pregnant woman was draping a tiny baby outfit over her round belly. Clay didn't bother to describe the scene any further.

We all looked at Clay once he finished his tale to judge his face, not that he would allow his visage to reveal any different from what he wanted us to believe. And he remained serious as he turned to Ms. Stine and said in his French detective dialect, "Mademoiselle Stine, we seem to have a criminal at large, oui?"

She tipped her head to one side in conviction and nodded, "Oui, Monsieur. It certainly seems so." She still had her arms crossed and looked at our table with a smile. Then, she silently walked away seemingly in thought. What is it about certain teachers that makes them more likable than others? I used to think that it was just if they were youthful or dressed in trendy clothes or spoke to us about current events in our lives. But I think it's the ones that try to understand us, who take a few minutes of their time to ask what is important to us and know how to be patient with our answers. Because, needless to say, school definitely isn't only about school.

I listened to Mindy talk to Harley about pursuing field hockey next school year while I prepared the bagel I brought for lunch. Harley seemed to be spending more time with us than with Alexis since field hockey was over. I still wondered if something happened between the girls or if Harley just decided we were easier to get along with. It made me glad to have Mindy's friendship, because she so effortlessly spread around an ease about her and made people want to know her. I benefitted from that, because I think that I, unintentionally, put up barriers with my quiet nature. I spent more time thinking and feeling where Mindy let it all out for all to hear and see. Most of the time that worked well.

I spread my bagel with whipped cream cheese and a couple of thin slices of tomato that I had wrapped separately in plastic. I like to top bagels and cream cheese with capers too, these little vinegary-soaked tree buds that burst with a lemony, salty flavor. But we didn't have any in the fridge when I was packing my lunch. After a few bites, I realized that I had forgotten to bring something to drink. Annoyed with myself, I got up from the lunch table to go over towards the cafeteria line. Time is so short at lunch, I was wasting it having to go get a bottle of water. Ridiculous, I said to myself. I pulled on my violet charm irritated. I didn't bother excusing myself so that I didn't interrupt Mindy's stream of consciousness on the subject of field hockey. I hastily covered my food with the plastic wrap and climbed over the stool away from the table.

I had to wind my way through small pockets of people waiting to be served and others just standing around, making it more difficult to slip through without trouble. I must've said "excuse me" five times behind a group of girls right in front of the refrigerated cooler I needed access to before I just nudged my shoulder in between them and reached in for a cold bottle of water.

Without warning, suddenly I was hurled backwards into the cashier's line a few feet away from the case of drinks, knocking two girls over and dropping my bottle on the floor. I was more surprised and embarrassed than hurt.

"Are you okay?" I asked the girls as we all tried to quickly stand as if nothing out of the ordinary had happened.

All of a sudden there was an angry overture of questions.

"What's your problem? Who's pushing? What are you doing?"

Only I had asked whether anyone was okay. I was ready to just let it go, pick up and pay for my water and just return to my cafeteria table and my small circle of friends. After all, I hadn't been the one to do anything on purpose. I felt awkward, but I was just in the wrong place at the wrong time. Or so I had thought.

The two girls who had also been in the way looked at me as I waited what seemed like a long minute. I don't think they knew what to say so they didn't say anything at all. But then Alexis' voice broke the unsure silence of the situation.

"I said," she repeated, taking her time with each word, "what's your problem?" Her face appeared inches from mine and even made the cashier look at her with a scowl of disapproval.

"Me? Nothing. I was just getting water and someone pushed me." I couldn't tell if my voice was strong and stable like I wanted it to sound or whether it stuttered with the pounding I could feel in my chest. I knew I hadn't instigated anything, and Alexis had just found a target. Me.

I grabbed the violet around my neck after handing the dollar still in my hand to the cashier. My knuckles were tight around the black cord as I attempted to breathe calmly and stave off the panic burning my insides.

"Nothing? I don't think so. You pushed me out of the way." She emphasized the words you and me in her accusation.

I immediately saw the lie rise in black smoke around her. I even stepped back in awe of its enormity, as if the smoke itself was real and capable of choking me. "You're lying," I said simply. I didn't mean to say it, but that's what I was thinking. It came right out of my mouth just as I pushed my violet underneath my shirt to hide it from the black smoke but also to lay it directly on my skin. I still had the bottle of water in my left hand.

"What?" she asked. "What did you say?" she asked incredulously, each word louder and louder.

There it was out there in the open already, so I stuck with it. "You are lying, and you know it." I decided to say this in finality and remove myself from the confrontation before my breathing came too fast and my mind would suffocate me. So, I clutched the bottle of water in my elbow and walked back towards the table where Mindy and Harley sat unaware of the confrontation I just experienced.

Mindy saw Alexis following me before I knew what was happening. I could see it in her eyes and on her skin as her melon colors turned quickly dark with mistrust and fear. Yellow and black streaks like a cat's eye looming in front of me. With a plan I didn't know I had, my right hand gave a swift turn of the top of the water bottle nestled in my left elbow, and I spun around and let the water fly from the bottle at whoever was behind me. The gush got Alexis mostly in the face, but the puddle it left didn't give her a chance to adjust to the slippery tile floor, and so she lost her footing in almost one instant movement of being splashed and falling to the floor on her back.

There was no question she'd be mad now. However, now I looked like the criminal. Mindy sat in shock at the sight in front of her, not knowing how to react, not knowing what could've spurred me to pour a bottle of water on this girl. Ms. Stine intervened immediately. She walked right up to me and put her hands on my arms as if to hold them down from doing anything else contemptible, which she knew was out of my character.

"What's going on here, Violet?" she asked with a more stern voice than she had ever directed at me before. I pulled away from her so that my back would not face Alexis. I didn't need a shield; I needed to see her. I wanted to make sure she wasn't going to get up and attack me from behind. I knew just then that her thoughts weren't to attack me. She was sitting on the floor slowly getting up so that she wouldn't slip in the water that surrounded her like a moat.

Ms. Stine dropped her hands from me as I had stepped out of the way, and she walked over and reached out to help up Alexis from the floor.

"Don't you touch me," Alexis yelled at the teacher. Now Alexis was treading on disrespect towards a teacher instead of fighting with another student.

"Fine, Alexis," Ms. Stine sniffed. She persisted in spite of annoyance at Alexis' nasty answer. "Are you all right? I was just trying to...."

As before, Alexis cut off Ms. Stine's sentence as she stood up. "I'm fine. How dare you believe her and not me!" Alexis accused Ms. Stine.

"I...I haven't done such a thing. I don't even know what happened," Ms. Stine said with confusion and a defensive note in her voice. She gathered herself and continued, "What I do know is we're all going to the principal's office right now." Ms. Stine almost yelled the last two words. I think she was frustrated, not mad, as a blue wave, deep and dark shrouded her head in suspicion. She knew there was more to this than what she saw. And I was determined to prove her right.

In the principal's office, Alexis and I had to wait to be seen, so she sat against one wall of the office while I sat in the alcove outside of the office. Unfortunately that meant that Alexis' side of the story would be the first one that was heard. That wasn't going to my advantage considering my side was the truth. About ten minutes later, Alexis had her opportunity to speak to the principal. The door was closed, and I tried to listen in but caught only raised phrases here and there, mostly with the word <u>she</u> in them. I guessed that meant I was the problem.

Then, Mr. Houseman opened the door to his office, let Alexis through and me inside. She, of course, whipped her head around visibly shunning me to further affirm my guilt.

"Just wait here," he said to Alexis. We left her in the seat I had occupied, and he closed his office door behind me.

I told Mr. Houseman the whole truth from my innocent snaking through the lines of people to get my water to my finding myself in a pile on the floor with two other innocent bystanders. I hoped that he'd see the whole thing as a misunderstanding and just forget about it. I didn't care whether Alexis served consequences for her actions or not. This whole time I was fighting to breathe against the heaviness of the violet weighing on my chest. I just needed this to all be over.

Ms. Stine had to go back to class in the meantime, so she couldn't even add her pieces of information. I knew that she didn't tolerate liars, but I also knew that she hadn't seen how Alexis had started the entire litany of events. I was going to have to give up on myself at the expense of the truth to just end this already. My violet was turning from the deepest hue of purple I had ever known to something foreign to me, something hateful that would make me unable to look in my mother's eyes or face my father as the daughter he'd always known. I hadn't even told Ms. Stine what had happened in the cafeteria. She just got to me first. Apparently, Mr. Houseman was going to talk to Ms. Stine after school today and question her. She was as much of an innocent bystander as those two girls standing at the drink cooler were.

There was that picture of Alexis and Ms. Stine in the cafeteria wading around in my brain again. I guessed this entire incident had played out in my imagination, but it didn't feel exactly right. I read the colors: the darkest indigo like the depths of the ocean where no light reaches and the suspicion rises in the night like a sliver of the moon. Waiting to be dismissed from Mr. Houseman's office, I played the piano in my head. The music grazed the air, a sharp slice whose cut lingers till dawn but threatens to return again. The music sounded like Mom's voice singing to me, and it calmed me just as much as it frustrated me. But I felt connected to her, even if just for a moment.

I know this message from Mom was right, but oh, so hard to take in the face of unkindness. It was on gray paper, the dull, infinite gray of the sky when the day shows no sign of letting up the rain.

My Little Violet,
Work hard for anything worthwhile. If it were easy, anyone could do it.

Chapter 8

AS I was walking home from the bus stop that afternoon, my phone chimed in receipt of a text message. I hoped it was good news as I was shuffling to the house as if my backpack was filled with every book I owned. My head hung low in defeat, feeling as if I'd disappointed myself, my father, and Ms. Stine in the process. I looked at the message box brightly glowing on my phone. It was from Mindy.

Alexis sez its her not u

Who's "her," I wondered. So I sent back one word.

Her?
Stine

My head filled with too many words to begin texting them back to Mindy. I gathered by the timing that she was on the school bus ride home, as I just was, and was able to hear any of the talk related to the incident in the cafeteria today. I couldn't help feeling embarrassed still for myself, and even a little for the way I made Alexis feel. But, if Alexis had blamed Ms. Stine for believing me and not giving her a chance to tell her side of the story, that is just conniving and badgering her. It makes me feel vengeful, like I want to go after Alexis and yell and scream in her face until she understands that what she has done is harassing and hurting someone else. Not to mention the fact that Ms. Stine is a great teacher. I would hate to be responsible for her getting into some sort of trouble because of me and my frustration at a girl who carries around a Slam Book and tells people what to do all the time.

I kept wondering why Alexis would bring Ms. Stine into this. Did it have something to do with those papers Alexis demanded from Ms. Stine when she stormed into our English period that one day? Or has Alexis always had a grudge against her for some reason? And there was that phone message Alexis played that night at Friendly's like it was some kind of evidence against Ms. Stine's teaching. It doesn't seem as if Alexis would treat a teacher that way because of a grade on a paper or a test or something like that, but I thought about it and granted I wouldn't put it past her with the way she's behaved around girls her own age. My mom would have said she acts like she's "entitled," that she deserves everything. People who expect life to owe them something without doing anything to deserve it. It made me grow with distaste for her. I didn't want to say I hated her; my parents did not raise me that way, but I felt a pounding in my head, and I began to notice my shoulders aching because I was hunching over so much, not realizing it was because my violet was hanging so heavily around my neck. Its midnight color was stark against my skin. Even though I hadn't looked at it with my eyes, I felt it punch a hollow between my lungs taking space away from the deep breaths I needed to be strong, to get through this mess I sensed wasn't over yet. I just wished I could ascertain a clearer picture in my mind instead of the knot in my stomach that was in my way.

I was so overwhelmed with this whole situation that I didn't even see that Breck was sitting in his Dad's car in front of Mrs. Suden's house listening to music on his phone until I had already gotten to my front door. He had rolled down the passenger window so that I could hear the rhythms spilling out and his voice calling my name over top of it. He yanked the buds out of his ears.

"Violet! Are you okay?" He yelled over top of his music.

I didn't want to meet his gaze. I still didn't know what kind of person Breck was, and I was sure that nothing sensible was going to pop out of my mouth in the mood I was in.

I had my phone in hand because I was going to call Mindy as soon as I walked inside and could drop the weight of my back pack on the floor and get a drink to soothe my panicky stomach. Dad always kept Italian bubbly mineral water around because it calms his stomach down too. Even though I wasn't in the right state to make conversation with Breck, it would've been impolite to just ignore him and go inside like I really wanted to do.

I swung my pack off my shoulder onto the ground at my feet and turned towards him with the most sincere smile I could muster. "Hi, Breck." I waved with the phone in my hand. That was all I could say. I leaned over to pick up my bag again and retrieved the house keys from the side pocket. I heard the car door slam shut so I knew to expect his arrival. I put my smile back on my face as best I could.

"Hey," he said, talking a little loudly over the music, a still, calm wreath of violet surrounding him. "You looked like you lost your dog or something. What's up?" he asked with concern, not familiarity.

I sighed not knowing what to say. Not knowing him yet, he seemed truly understanding. "It wasn't a good day is all," I offered. As if Mindy knew what I was thinking, my phone chimed again with a text message, but I didn't want to be rude to Breck, so I ignored it.

"Well, it's not over yet," he said. "There's room for improvement, right?" He seemed so upbeat and was trying so hard to make me feel better even though he didn't know who I was or what I had done. "I'm waiting for my dad while he shows some people through the house." He gestured towards Mrs. Suden's house, and I noticed a champagne-colored four-door parked behind his dad's car in the driveway. Although he hadn't actually asked me a question, I could tell he was waiting for an affirmative or negative as to whether I'd be willing to fill his empty time.

We were already at the stoop of our porch so I asked him if he wanted to come inside for a drink.So he followed me inside and even carried into the house my backpack by the black nylon loop at its top.

"You can drop it there," and I pointed to the floor in front of the hall coat closet. I looked him in the eye and said, "Thanks." For a second time, I felt like I meant more with that one word than I actually said. It was nice to have some company now, although I would have spent the next hour on the phone with Mindy as if she were here in my house. Another text arrived on my phone, so I pushed the tiny button to turn off the phone and left it on the table in the front hall where Dad drops his keys and I'll put the mail, if I've remembered to get it.

I didn't know if he'd want to see the house, but I wasn't prepared to show him all around without knowing where exactly I had left all of my personal items, even the not so personal ones. So instead we went into the kitchen, and he agreed to have a glass of Italian mineral water with me, even though he hadn't ever had it before. He said it was like drinking air with some fizz in it. He was probably right, but I felt my stomach relax once the bubbles settled. We sat at the kitchen table so that he could see when his dad was preparing to leave his house showing. There was an easy view of the neighbor's from our window over the sink.

Instead of talking about my day, Breck told me about his. He actually goes to a private academy across the river. His parents are both realtors, and although he didn't say so, I knew he thought that he didn't want me to judge him as if they were some snobby rich people who could afford to send him there. He never said whether he liked it or not, but it seemed like that was all he had ever known. I was trying hard to listen to what he said and not confuse myself with his thoughts too.

"Well, has my boring life gotten you to forget yours? At least you've got some excitement, right?" he laughed at himself.

I laughed along with him. I appreciated him for trying to make me feel better even though I wasn't offering any details about my woes. Just as I was getting ready to give up the story, his dad appeared in the driveway next door. Breck got up from the table and walked over to the refrigerator where my dad and I hung a shopping list on a pad with a magnet on the back. He wrote down his cell phone number.

"Got to go, but call me sometime if you ever forget how exciting your life is. I'm happy to talk you out of it." He actually walked back over to me and gave me a little friendly pat on the back. He started walking through the hall to the door. I followed him out trying to think of something to say other than "thanks" again. He said, "Don't drink too much of that bubble water. See ya'." He opened the door himself and walked outside.

"Thanks, uh...Breck." I laughed at my own thoughtlessness. "It was really nice talking to you." At least I added that. I sighed at myself and closed the door. I wasn't sure if I felt more stupid and useless than before for just that moment. I grabbed my glass of water and took the last sip. I looked at the empty glass and let out a little laugh. I guess I felt somewhat better, at least my stomach did. My violet was still uncommonly dark when I pulled it out of the collar of my top. It made me unsure of the relief I was feeling. I decided it was time to call Mindy before Dad got home. Although I knew somehow that I was ignoring something else.

I dreaded having to tell Dad about today's events. And talking to Mindy didn't really enlighten the situation at all. She didn't know whether Alexis also had detention, only that she was blaming Ms. Stine. I wasn't positive of his reaction, and I thought he'd understand that I didn't start anything. He'd nod his head expecting that I learned my lesson. I just felt like I was disappointing him. I wasn't going to keep it from him; I don't like keeping secrets. Plus, I was going to be arriving home late from school tomorrow due to the punishment.

I figured that I'd make a hearty dinner for us to take my mind off the whole scene. I took some frozen turkey meatballs out of the freezer and put them in a shallow saucepan with a jar of spaghetti sauce. I added a packet of Italian spices that my mom used to say was her secret ingredient, stirred in the powder to cover the meatballs, and covered the pan to simmer the sauce over low heat till Dad came home. I took out a box of angel hair pasta and left in on the counter. I looked out the window as I washed some lettuce in a strainer over the sink and saw Cropsie walk by carrying pine garland over his shoulder and a snarl of Christmas lights dragging on the ground behind him. Instead of being startled by his presence, I was reminded that the Jewish holiday of Hanukkah was here and the time had come for my idea that I had come up with at Hershey's Sweet Lights. I dropped the strainer in the sink and went over to the kitchen desk to pull out the calendar. We should have already been lighting the candles on the menorah, but we still had tonight, tomorrow night and Wednesday night left to make eight. I can't believe that I had let the holiday slip my mind, especially since Dad had just been to temple services last weekend.

So tonight was the fifth night of Hanukkah. I was glad that I had started a good dinner tonight too. Last year's holiday season was hard without Mom for the first time. We hadn't celebrated Hanukkah and didn't do much of anything to honor her or to fill our own empty hearts. So, I didn't want to let another holiday go by like that.

When Dad came home, I had the table set for dinner, and I had gathered rose-colored candles in honor of my mother. I told Dad about my day, and he nodded his head just as I had expected. We lit the Hanukkah candles after we ate the pasta with meatballs and a salad with Italian dressing. We said the blessings over the candles in quiet, melodic voices, and I know that Dad was missing Mom just as I was. I carefully carried the menorah with its burning candles into the parlor and led him to the chair beside the piano. He sat down and helped me set the menorah on the wide part of the sill of the front bay window next to the chair so they could shine outside while I played one of his favorite songs for him as his Hanukkah present. I don't do that often, so I know he really appreciated it—the song is "Sunrise, Sunset" from *Fiddler on the Roof*. Under the hazy shine of the rose candles burning in the window, I didn't want Dad to be sad, but he looked out at the orange and pink rings of the sun setting low in the sky behind the neighbors' houses across the street. As I played, I felt a connection with Mom as if I were bridging a gap. I wished I could hear her voice. We were celebrating the miracle of Hanukkah—it made me feel better in light of the day that I'd had. Even though it was with mixed feelings for both Dad and me, it was a good evening. I needed it to restore a better day tomorrow.

That night I had trouble sleeping. I felt like I was in that dreamy state of wakeful sleep where my inclinations were spilling into the dream, somewhere in between control and imagination. I was picturing the neighborhood in *To Kill A Mockingbird*, southern and simple. Old small houses with crooked porches and dry bushes skirting them. Lattice swings creaking on their metal chains hanging in front of the shuttered windows. Mindy and I were walking past the houses, dark inside and empty, but they didn't intimidate us. I felt nervous walking by them even while Mindy seemed confident. We saw other children, younger than we were, kicking stones around and playing tag; they seemed to be unaware of the emptiness of the neighborhood. Suddenly, our faces were whipped by wind and dust, leaves and flower petals of all different colors, making it hard to see in front of us. I barely could make out a figure down the dirt road, but I couldn't distinguish more than a shadow. In fact, as we approached it, I wanted to tell Mindy that we should turn around, go the other way. At the same time, Mindy was heading towards it faster, leaning into the wind. I was pulling her back, trying to yell, although the words were lost in the rush pushing and pulling us. Whatever my words were weren't even clear to me, but I began to feel that nervousness grow into panic, my violet suffocating me around my throat and forcing me to turn back. To run. I saw streams of violet flying towards her, and I was stretching to reach it and Mindy. I felt like I was risking everything, and I couldn't hang on in the flurry of the wind. She disappeared from me. I fell backwards into the dirt with just my violet clutched to my chest. It was dark. I opened my eyes. It was dark. It was the darkness of my bedroom, and my breathing was too fast and too loud. I rolled over to look at my mother's picture in the glow of my phone, yet seeing her didn't give me the comfort it usually did. I swallowed a sip of water from the glass next to the picture frame to calm me, set down the glass and picked up my phone. I guess after cleaning up from dinner and waiting until the menorah's lights had burned out, I hadn't remembered to check the messages on my phone before plugging it in to charge as I got in bed.

I saw the number eight blink on my phone. It was almost five o'clock in the morning, but I sat up with a start and looked at the list of messages. Only one had been from Mindy shortly after our conversation right after getting home off the bus. It had said, "Call me."

The others were from a number I did not recognize. My fingers tightened around my phone in fear and surprise. The sip of water I had taken churned in my stomach along with the trace of the bad dream I had. I ran my index finger along the cord to stretch it away from my neck. It wasn't tight, but it felt like it. The violet flashed with a dark red shimmering through the petals like blood through veins from its center to its edges, and it seemed as if violet colors were flickering around me. Then, I took a deep breath and scrolled through the messages:

Ur a liar
Ur a fake
Ur a pest
Ur a coward
Ur a fool
Ur a witch
Ur a suck up

I didn't fall back asleep that morning before dawn. I watched the sun rise from my bedroom window thinking about what I should do. I had a strong feeling this was just the beginning, and there were no colors to help me sort it out.

The words stood out on a sheet of electric violet paper as smooth as a fleece blanket. I wanted to crumple it up in a soft ball and throw it away quietly. Unfortunately, I would not be able to do that.

My Little Violet,
Keep your friends close and your enemies closer. Unless it's time to protect your friends.

Chapter 9

I was dreading the rest of the week of school, but at least I knew that this was it for a couple weeks while we had Winter Break ahead, except for the Cobalt Valley Winter Solstice which was scheduled for this Wednesday evening at the high school. Its designated night is December 21st, the shortest day and therefore the longest night of the year. The elementary schools, the middle school, and the high school are all invited to listen to a variety of the schools' musical groups sing Christmas carols and play holiday music. Some parents and students who usually help out the choirs and the band with their equipment sell souvenir t-shirts and knit caps to raise money for the spring musical. Some of the teachers show up to sell baked goods, hot coffee and hot chocolate; they mill around chatting with everyone and enjoying the concert-style evening. In the middle school choir group, we had been rehearsing songs for the evening since practically the first week of school. Now I wasn't positive I was permitted to perform. Either way, I should be looking forward to the plans for Wednesday, as they'll help me pass the night without Dad.

Mindy was especially excited to go because Austin had mentioned something to me in English class about going, so she thought it might be a good opportunity to strike up a conversation with him. She kept texting me in the mornings before school to remind me to bring it up with him while we were working on our trial project together in class. That's one of the nice things about working on group projects in Ms. Stine's class—we get time to socialize while we're working, and I think we learn while we're having fun. Austin had assured me that he was going to go to Winter Solstice because the football team was expected to support the band and vice versa. So, I figured he'd show up with some of the other players and hang around in the lobby near the food.

My mind was occupied with the strange text messages I had received, although I was pretty sure who sent them. Mindy told me not to delete them as they were "evidence" in case something happened. It made me remember the dream that had initially woken me up early this morning. Although I had told Mindy about the messages on my phone, I did not want to tell her about the dream. The dream disturbed me even more because I remembered the colors. Mindy wasn't melon anymore. There was no colors to read, no thoughts to listen for.

I passed Mindy as she was leaving Ms. Stine's class and I was entering. We stopped in the hallway against the lockers to catch up with each other.

Mindy started off right away with Austin on her mind. "Hey, Vi. You should try to see if Austin wants to go to the mall before Winter Solstice. I want to go to look for something to wear New Year's Eve. You'll go with me, right?"

"Yeah, sure. Dad's not home, so I'll just go home with you. If that's okay...," I trailed off, trying not to sound as if I preferred it any other way. "We can grab some dinner there too unless you wanted to do something else."

"Nope, sounds perfect. My mom will take us. See ya' at lunch." She left in a twirl of melon, her pointed brown boots clopping down the hall.

I was glad to have plans each and every Wednesday, so going to the mall was a good a plan as any for me. I didn't shop very often, although I liked to. I tried to ignore the urge I had to check my phone for any more offensive messages before class started. That's all I needed on top of getting in trouble for throwing water on Alexis in the cafeteria. I'd get my phone taken for using it in class, and then Dad would have to make a trip into the office to retrieve it. That certainly wouldn't make him happy, as that would be more of a deliberate delinquent move. It wouldn't be the same as defending myself against someone else's unwelcome threats. At least not as far as Dad knew at this point.

I shook away the thought of more texts and focused on Ms. Stine's journal entry for the day. She was busy checking off reading logs around the room as we all wrote for a few minutes about our approach to life. Was I cynical, optimistic or practical? This was Ms. Stine's way to get a few vocabulary words in, for sure, but I thought it required a rather complicated answer. I was a little bit of all three, but I supposed that was her point.

I was cynical in that I didn't always think that I was going to make something of myself, especially now without my mother in my life. I was optimistic when I realized that I had things in my life worthwhile and people that I appreciated—Dad, Mindy, even Austin, Ms. Stine, and maybe even Breck. I was a good pianist, and I got good grades in school. I was far from perfect. I keep to myself and don't ask for help, even when I need it. I probably don't come across as a very warm person either, but I think that people trust me and believe in my integrity. The worst things I can remember that I've ever done besides throwing water at Alexis was walking away from Mom in a store once when I was around five, and she got really mad because I knew better. And, I lied about the panic attacks I had as I was growing up. My parents expected me to share everything with them because I was their only object of attention. But, as we realized my ability to read the colors around people and my phobia of crowds, there began to be those secrets that made me special—the same things that made me cynical of people and everything around me. Because of the colors and what they meant.

As I was thinking about it, I guess out of the three adjectives, I'm the least practical, so I left that one out of my journal entry. I don't do it on purpose, but I'm dependent on the colors I see around me to guide me. I haven't made major decisions about my life based on those colors, but I've found myself listening to them more and more as I've gotten older. I think I have an acute sense of intuition, too, but that definitely has nothing to do with practicality. I hate to judge others based on my visions though, because I'm not always convinced that the colors show me the real truth or whether it's part of my own thoughts. In fact, I probably lied about the colors I saw too, sometimes, when my parents asked me if I saw anything unusual or if I seemed anxious. I don't remember, but I probably did. I keep the colors to myself now. Dad doesn't ask about them, and besides Mindy and maybe Austin and a few others I've gone to school with since we were in first grade, I doubt anyone even thinks about what I have seen in the air around us. Which is just the way I like it.

I turned my attention back to English class and finishing our preparations for the trial we were going to start tomorrow. Austin and I had written out our statements of defense. I actually found myself getting nervous thinking about having to speak in front of the whole class and trying to be persuasive on top of it. We're using the dialogue and events from the court scene in *To Kill A Mockingbird*, so it's not as if we have to rewrite everything, but it makes it much more real when saying it aloud. I think putting myself in the place of the defense lawyer is also what makes me nervous—pretending to be responsible for someone else's freedom still feels like a great responsibility. I wanted to actually practice the words coming out of my mouth to make me feel less nervous about it.

Time in class was waning, so I had to hurry to finish reading my piece to Austin. I was starting to pick up the pace. I glanced up at the clock above the door and kept reading from the paper I held in both hands, when the last person I wanted to see strolled in the door.

I turned my back to the door and continued reading to Austin. He looked up and noticed why I had shifted my back towards him; without uttering a word, he stood up with his broad shoulders and shielded me from her view. Even though I had lost my concentration, I finished.

Austin said, "Sounds great. We're gonna blow the prosecution away!" He laughed but I felt like he had confidence in our side. "No, really. It sounds great, Vi."

I nodded. I believed in our position that we were presenting. I just was a little uncomfortable speaking to an audience. We started packing up our things as Ms. Stine was announcing to the class that it was time to do so. I tried to look up through my lashes so I wasn't being obvious in my curiosity as to Alexis' presence.

Alexis almost interrupted her and spoke as soon as Ms. Stine finished addressing the class. "Ms. Stine, do you have those papers for me?"

Ms. Stine answered her politely but firmly. "Excuse me, Alexis. I'll be with you in a moment." Ms. Stine crossed in front of Alexis with her answer and walked over to one of the other teams of students who was preparing for our trial tomorrow. One of the girls had raised her hand, so it appeared that Ms. Stine was answering her question, although I couldn't hear her.

Alexis crossed her arms and actually starting tapping her foot on the tile floor with a flat but irritating sound. Ms. Stine ignored it purposely; I could tell. I was watching how Ms. Stine handled Alexis' entrance since this wasn't the first time our class was interrupted. After a short conversation with the group, she walked past Alexis again over to her desk by the windows. Without saying a word, Ms. Stine took out a manila folder from a metal organizer on her desk and pulled out a short pile of paper. She handed it to Alexis who took it from her hands with a glare in her eye. It seemed like she was willing Ms. Stine to say something. The silent pause was obvious to the entire class.

I was waiting for Alexis to at least mumble a "thanks," but instead she turned around with a swish of the papers by her side and disappeared without even a second thought about the impression she had left, not only on Ms. Stine but on all of us. A suspicious wave of dark blue, almost black, billowed in the air behind her. I saw Alexis' bad intentions becoming clearer now. It wasn't going to be just Ms. Stine she affected, but all of us.

"See you in January, Alexis," Ms. Stine called after her with sincerity in her voice. I wondered if it was real. I expected a mistrustful dark yellow sunset to emanate around her, but there was no captivating color surrounding Ms. Stine. Knowing how much I admired her, I was a little confused that I couldn't read her right now. Because I wanted to help her, even though I wasn't sure I knew exactly how I could.

I dismissed the whole issue and was preparing to leave for lunch when Ms. Stine continued; I wasn't sure if she was telling us or just finishing her thought aloud.

"She'll be joining this class in January."

I was taken aback almost in shock. My blood rushed to my head so fast it made me dizzy, and I had to sit back down in my chair even though we were all getting ready to leave class at Ms. Stine's word. I tried to clear my head with logical thoughts, like why it should matter whether Alexis was in this class at all and why I let someone like her get the best of me.

As if Austin heard my thoughts, he bent over and spoke softly in my ear. "It doesn't matter, Vi. Why do you let her bother you so much?" His question was rhetorical in its tone and was accompanied by his sliding my books on top of his and hooking his other arm in mine to literally lift me out of my seat. "Come on. I'll walk you to lunch."

Ms. Stine had dismissed us, although I hadn't heard her words. The usual chatter in the hallways, especially before lunch, droned in my ears like wind rushing in the car windows on the highway.

On top of the tension from English class, I wasn't even allowed to go to lunch today and be able to tell Mindy everything. My punishment was lunch detention for the remainder of the week. I had to eat in one of the empty rooms in the main office. I tried to tell Austin this as he walked me to the cafeteria, but I couldn't get the words out. My brain was buzzing. I tried to urge my free hand that wasn't locked into Austin's to raise my violet to my lips to take a deep cleansing, calming breath. I wasn't able until I saw Mindy spot our entrance to the cafeteria. The flicker of green caught me off guard coming from Mindy's stable melon, and I realized that jealousy rose in her instinctually for just an instant. I was able to inhale and exhale the violet's effects on me that released me from needing Austin's support while reassuring Mindy that I wasn't trying to lure Austin's attentions away from her. In fact it worked rather well in Mindy's favor.

"Hey, Violet, are you all right?" she paused. With a broad smile, she put her hand on Austin's arm as he was helping me onto a stool at our usual table. "Hi...what's going on?"

"That girl, uhh...Alexis, I think, is her name," Austin explained. Mindy nodded and rolled her eyes. "She'll be moving into our class after Winter Break, or so Ms. Stine says."

"What great news!" Mindy said sarcastically, and she exaggerated the statement by throwing her arms up in the air like a cheer.

"If you're in good hands now, Violet, I'm gonna head over...," Austin gestured with his thumb towards the table with his friends and teammates.

"Of course," Mindy answered him quickly and touched his

arm ever so lightly again. "Thanks for helping my friend. Oh, see you tomorrow night," she added.

"Yeah, no problem." Austin smiled at Mindy, and I thought I caught some sparks in Austin's golden shadow. He walked away.

Mindy sat right down without a moment to waste. "What a great idea to get Austin to talk to me, Violet. You're such a great best friend." She hugged me in her glee, so I didn't really have any need to tell her it wasn't planned.

What I had to do before I got into more trouble was go get lunch as quickly as I could and make my way to the office. I reminded Mindy that I had lunch detention, and I actually began to see the good in it, for today at least. I went through the cafeteria line, grabbed a turkey sandwich, and went up to pay. I glanced around the drink cooler like a tiger casing the meadow for the lion. I picked up a bottle of strawberry water and paid for my lunch. The quickest way to the office was out in the hallway instead of trying to weave in and out of the tables in the cafeteria, so I walked that way finally feeling like my head had cleared and my pulse had slowed to normal. I narrowed my eyes and looked behind me, feeling like I was being followed. It was a strange sensation in my stomach. I figured it was just that I hadn't realized how hungry I was.

I sat down with relief in the tiny room that the office secretary pointed out to me. Just to be alone in a quiet place was what I needed right now. I ate my sandwich and lay my chin down on top of my hands on the small old desk that was stuck in the corner. I was able to look outside the lone rectangular window that opened out with a levered handle. I enjoyed the minutes of peace and then realized that I had no idea what time it was so that I could get to my last class, History with Mindy, on time. Even though we weren't supposed to use cellphones during the school day, I didn't think anyone would catch me checking the time on it, so that's what I did.

I didn't notice the time. Instead I noticed the number of text messages having silently crept up on me like that tiger treading through the tall grass of the meadow. However, I wasn't the predator. I was the prey.

The sandwich I had eaten gurgled in my stomach and rose into my throat. I opened the window without even thinking and was able to stick my head out far enough to let it go outside. I took deep breaths of the cold winter air into my lungs. I pulled my head back inside to take a few sips from my bottle of water, closed my eyes, and brought my violet to my lips. This time I did kiss it, softly and slowly, willing it to give me the strength to get through the panic and the guidance to stop it from happening.

I hadn't heard anyone enter, but when I opened my eyes, Clay was standing there with his jovial grin and his cardboard-colored hair sticking up in the front. I think it was on purpose. He opened his eyes wider when he saw that I wasn't feeling well.

"When Mindy and I noticed you weren't in History class, we figured you didn't have any way to tell time in this," he looked around the room for a moment and shrugged his arms and repeated, "thees, prizen cell. I, ze private eye," he actually pointed to his eye as he continued in his French detective accent, "am here to rescue you." He opened his arms wide as if he were a hero. It sure felt like he was though.

"Thanks, Clay, you're my hero," and I gingerly stood up from my chair and swallowed, trying to force a brave smile.

He let me lean on him without hesitation as if he were meant to be my crutch. We threw away my lunch trash on the way out, and I took another sip of water on our way down the hall to history class. We hadn't said much until we neared the classroom.

Clay said, "I have just the solution to your problem."

I looked at him confused, as I wasn't sure whether he really knew what my problem was. I could've just had a stomach bug. My forehead wrinkled up as I waited for him to clarify.

"Kill her with kindness," he said. And with that he let me go, and I walked into class as if floating into my seat. He followed me soundlessly so that we didn't disturb the students who were working quietly in pairs. I began to sense a calming in the colors and my violet became a crystal clear purple as I felt more in control. I noted that the violet hues settled around Clay as well. I was trying to recall whether I had ever seen Clay's colors before, and the funny thing was, I didn't think that it mattered.

I understood Mom's note as frustrating as it might be. It plagued me on a dull, dry sheet of paper that was so brittle, it felt like baby's breath, the tiny stems and flowers that protect us from the roses' thorns.

My Little Violet,
Be civil. Respect for others comes back to you.

Chapter 10

ON the bus ride home I sent text messages in reply to the first of the two sets of offensive messages I had received during the day. I didn't bother blocking my number as I guessed the recipient knew the number that she had targeted in the first place. I hadn't told Clay or Mindy that I was going to reply, but after Clay's suggestion, I thought it was a good idea. If I was stirring the pot and inciting more messages, then so be it. I was going to keep at it. I was not prepared to confront Alexis, so in my mind, this was the only way that I could retaliate and feel like I had some control over the situation. I knew I couldn't control her, assuming, of course, that she was the one bullying me with her unkind words, to say the least.

When I got home that afternoon from school, I went straight to the piano bench and sat down. With no intention, I began to play a melody that was in my head. The notes just came to me. Suddenly, I stopped playing and ran up to my bedroom closet. All of this time I had tried to push away the feeling in my heart that I knew there was more to the colors than what was tangible. I didn't just see the colors; I read them. I didn't just hear the music inside my mind; I played it. I retrieved the dried rose and violets from its hiding place inside the wall and carried them downstairs on top of the book in a grasp so tender that I was barely touching them. I laid the flowers gently on top of the piano's walnut-finished case, careful not to lose any of the petals in my placement. I laid out the thick book on the ledge for the music books to rest and opened it to the middle so that it would sit there and let me read the notes without the pages collapsing back together. I was beginning to recover from Alexis' tormenting as I returned to playing the song I had begun.

I had closed my eyes and tried to balance the evil intentions I associated with her actions and the color I associated with Alexis— for now, it was red. I saw the music match the color in my head, but it wasn't fitting quite right. I still felt bullied and scared. I didn't know how I was going to deal with this; I couldn't take going to school every day if I was going to continue feeling this way. But I hated that she was pushing me around and making me feel this way—so worthless and weak.

The book. Why wasn't I looking at the book? It was full of music. There didn't appear to be song titles, but each page was a different color, a range of shades and textures to match almost any personality or essence or emotion I had ever encountered. And each page was lined with music, staff after staff filling the pages with flowing arcs of song that I could hear in my head before even playing them out on the keys in front of me. I carefully turned the pages. Some were so delicate and thin. Some were old and worn but tough to the touch. I would have to play for months if I paged through them all.

I thought I would try a red one to see if it would make things better with Alexis. I knew I was reading her correctly, so I found a page that was a fiery red, like the embers of a burnt log, red and glowing in waves below the white ash of the wood that would fly away as dust if a strong wind blew hard enough to extinguish the flames. It was exactly what I wanted to do. I lost time for I concentrated on the music with all I could muster.

This time my playing was interrupted by the phone ringing. Its melody seemed to sound suspiciously like the song I was playing, but I didn't acknowledge the similarity. I unzipped the front pocket of my backpack and pulled out my phone hoping that this was not another threat. To my pleasant surprise, it was Breck calling. I recognized the number from his writing it on the pad on the fridge, not because I had ever called him before nor received one from him. A faint tickle started in my stomach, but it made me smile instead of lose my breath completely.

"Hello," I answered, trying not to show recognition of the caller in my voice.

"Hi, Violet, it's Breck."

"What's up?" My voice sounded steady and cool so far.

"Not much. Just checking in on you. Hope you're doing better ...."

That made my throat catch. "It's really nice of you—I'm good, yeah, much better. Sorry I never called you to let you know." I glanced down at my feet, a little embarrassment flushing my cheeks with rosy splotches. I was glad he couldn't see me. "I...um...well, tomorrow night I'm going to the high school for a holiday celebration type thing...with Mindy and...you could come too...if you wanted to...if you're not busy or anything." I couldn't believe I was able to draw out this confidence, but I felt like Clay's words earlier boosted my self-esteem.

"Yeah, definitely. I mean, I'll go...I'm not busy," Breck said with a hint of surprise in his voice. "Where can I meet you?"

"Some of us are going to the mall first. To hang out and eat, probably, so you could meet us there. Like five...or, how about six?" I remembered that Mindy's mom was taking us around five o'clock, so this way we'd be sure to have separated from her by that point and could explore on our own.

"I will text you when I get there so we can find a place to meet up. Ok?" He sounded as excited as I was feeling.

"Perfect. See you tomorrow. Six o'clock," I said.

He said good-bye and hung up. I was still looking at my phone in my hands, standing in the front hall leaning up against the archway that separated it from the parlor. I instinctually placed my hand over my violet on my chest, for once with a good feeling, like it was continually becoming wiser, a clearer pool of violet color like the sky at dusk. I looked into the parlor at the piano with the dried flowers on top and walked back in to finish playing the song. I put my cellphone on top of the upright next to the flowers. I felt strength pour through my arms and my fingers down to the keys and closed my eyes, lost in the spray of colors I created with the rise and fall of the musical notes.

As sure as I was of anything, a grainy vision of my mother appeared above the piano as I played, and her words spoke to me within the notes of the song. My eyes still squeezed shut and my violet glowed around my neck. I connected the energy from the music and the flowers to project this display before me.

Her voice was almost singing, "The hardest thing I ever did was to leave you, but I did it to save you and your gift, and because I love you and your father so much. Follow the music of the colors, my Little Violet."

I was stunned with the notion of having just heard my mother's voice after so long. Instead of panicking me, it released me. I believed in this apparition—I couldn't have imagined it for it filled my being. I felt even stronger knowing her presence was still in my reach. It made me wonder whether she could ever return to our lives.

When I opened my eyes and stopped playing to make sense of my existence, I felt Dad's presence behind me. I turned around on the bench and saw him leaning with his arms crossed against the archway where I had just been standing. He didn't tell me whether he had only heard me play or whether he saw what I saw or whether he saw and heard all of it. He turned away and called to me as he walked into the kitchen.

"Violet, help me make dinner. It's time."

Not knowing how to react to the visit Mom had just made, we began preparing dinner routinely. Dad poured himself a glass of wine, a red zinfandel, which had a murky red to it that shimmered with purple and black. He didn't usually drink much, but I supposed he had something to tell me. I let him take the lead and didn't ask any questions. The colors of the wine mingled with his own blue energy that helped him stay focused on work, even though it conveyed to me that he's still living with sadness. We talked about Mom while Dad sliced tomatoes and I put the burgers under the broiler and set the table. It's hard to remember what life was like—not because I don't have memories, but because we have had to change roles to include the things she used to do. And that makes me miss her so much more.

Standing with his back against the kitchen counter, Dad cut slivers of cheese from a block of white cheddar and popped a wedge in his mouth with a sip of wine. He seemed a little more relaxed with that, and the story flowed. What he presumed I had just done was unleashed the power of the violet, he told me, by playing the music from the book I found. He guessed that I was becoming more open to my gift and that could have carved a window for Mom to be able to communicate with me.

"I wasn't positive that you'd ever be capable of doing it, but since you have, you have a dilemma in front of you." He spoke with uncertainty but hope in his voice. He touched my hand then before I opened the oven door to take out the broiled burgers. I looked at him with the seriousness he was demanding. "The women in your mother's family are strong, Violet. And you are one of the strongest. Your mother told me so. Before she had to leave, disappear from our lives. But she said there was a way, a possibility you'd figure it out because you are so smart. She couldn't tell me much; otherwise, she knew you'd read my thoughts and start looking for her."

I opened my mouth to ask a question, but my thoughts were jumbled up in my head. Dad tilted his head to the side, obviously thinking but nothing I could listen to. He sat down at the table, as

I laid the hot burgers on the open rolls on our plates with a server. "You have a gift, Violet, and with that comes a responsibility." He sighed and looked up at the ceiling. "A responsibility not just to your mother, but to her mother, and her mother." He emphasized the word <u>her</u> in each phrase, which illuminated for me the reason I had never known my grandmother.

"But how?" It seemed as if my question should've been longer, but I didn't even know where to begin.

"You have to use the colors you see. I don't know how you do that, how you even see the colors, so I don't know how to help you, but I will do whatever I can, Violet." He cleared his throat, but the rest didn't come out in his clear voice. "I don't want to lose you, too."

I must've had doubt on my face. My forehead must have wrinkled up. I slid the violet on its cord back and forth subconsciously while my mind was working. I began to eat slowly trying to figure out what I can do that would be so powerful. Most of the time, I don't even realize the colors I see—they're just a part of life for me.

Our dinner was unhurried and quiet, and we inevitably talked about Mom and memories we had of her. Dad was telling me how special he knew she was right away, how he was drawn to her beauty and her kindness to others. She loved working in the flower shop because even if her customers were buying flowers for a sad occasion, the flowers healed their feelings even if just for that moment. That was how Mom had used her gift—matching the energy she saw in others with the right flower. And, Mom communicated through her music but loved to teach her skills, hoping that she could incite a love of music in others. I considered those facets of my mother, understanding at first only my own joy when I played the piano. She always had encouraging words, and with her students, she would give them stickers that they could accumulate and turn in for little prizes. They liked her for her kind and patient manner. Dad and I finished talking, but I continued to mull over the confident person my mother was and what that might mean to me now so that I can bring us back together. That sounded so incredible to me. And it scared me too.

After cleaning up from dinner, I told Dad I was going up to take a bath for a change, to sit and think for a while. I knew I wouldn't sleep very well tonight.

I had no plan, but I tired myself out trying to think of one.

In some strange way I felt nothing like myself and more like myself than I ever had in the morning. I checked Mom's face in her photograph, and, looking exactly the same as always, I didn't worry that much else had changed after my vision last night. Getting ready for school today was also more motivating because of the after-school activities we had planned. I was drawn to wearing one of my cable-knit sweaters this morning that was thick and warm and covered me in my favorite purple. The yarn was speckled with silver and white and was soft on my skin. It made me feel lifted up and energized. I added a pair of skinny black pants because our trial was starting today in English class, and I thought it was appropriate to dress professionally. And, the pants were comfortable and nice to wear tonight too. I was allowed to sing in the chorus performance at Winter Solstice, even though I had been serving lunch detentions for my consequence. The singing was fun and not as personal to me as the piano playing. It felt good to look forward to something fun for a change.

Looking in the mirror at myself, I silently promised myself that I was going to figure this out and not let down my parents. I looked back at Mom's picture on my nightstand, smiled back at her smile, and flipped off my bedroom light.

Running downstairs to catch Dad for breakfast, I wanted to be sure to spend some time this morning with him before he left, since it was Wednesday, and he'd be working late. And, I was trying to decide how much to tell Mindy about what happened yesterday, so I thought I'd see what he thought.

When I came into the kitchen, thinking I had beat him there, Dad already had his things by the door including a suitcase. He had prepared me the other half of the grapefruit he was eating, and a few slices of toast were buttered but cold on a plate in front of him.

"Good morning, sweetheart. Sit down and eat with me," he said. "I got an email early this morning, and...," with an aggravated shake of his head, he decided to cut the story short. "Anyway, I'm going to have to stay over in D.C. tonight. Do you think you can stay over at Mindy's?"

"I'm sure of it. We had already planned to go to the mall after school with her mom for dinner and shopping before Winter Solstice tonight at the high school." I always miss Dad when he's gone, but today was going to be so busy anyway that it wouldn't be as hard tonight.

"Oh, good. Sorry for the last minute," he said as he pushed away from the table and took his dishes to the sink. He kissed me on top of the head and went over to the coffee pot to fill up his travel cup. As if Mom reminded him with the coffee maker, he said, "Please be careful. Stay with Mindy. Don't go off on your own at the mall or at the concert."

"I won't, Dad. Promise." I stood up with a piece of toast in my hand to get something to drink out of the refrigerator. Even though I felt a little hesitant, I wanted to give Dad a big hug. He must've sensed my need for his protective arms around me and took me in his arms. He gave me another kiss on my forehead. "Thanks, Dad. I love you. You be careful, too." I broke the serious mood with my last comment.

"I love you, too. See you tomorrow after school. Text me to let me know how everything's going, if you want to," he said as he gathered his bags and coat and coffee mug.

I opened the door to the garage for him and said good-bye. I continued eating my breakfast and cleaned up the kitchen quickly to get out the door to catch the bus to school. I almost forgot about making sure I was welcome to stay over at Mindy's. It bothered me that Dad got frustrated with his work, but it forced me to take care of myself, and that wasn't an entirely bad thing. I sent Mindy a text asking her, which was really a formality. While I waited for her response, I had already run back upstairs to my bedroom and began shoving a pair of jeans, a long-sleeved tee, something to sleep in and my toiletries into a white canvas tote bag that had "Violet" embroidered in purple on the side. Mindy replied by the time I was putting on my coat to leave. She was excited about today as well, and my staying over at her house was a bonus.

It was going to be a long, interesting day, I thought, as I walked out to catch the bus with my extra bag over my shoulder. This must be how Dad feels when he's leaving for work in the morning. I forgot to bring lunch, I thought to myself. My mind was definitely preoccupied with so many competing needs. I wiggled my bags through the tall, narrow doorway of the school bus and gripped the railing to help myself up the steps. I wedged down the aisle, sat down in the first open seat, and dropped everything in a tangled pile. Yes, a long, interesting day, I thought as I looked out the window at the morning sky unfolding with pink.

This paper was like blood, a frightening dark blue-red that scared me with its intensity and made me suspicious of what was to come, although the message was promising.

My Little Violet,
Do it for ten minutes. If you feel like stopping then stop,
but chances are, you'll keep going. Study. Play the piano.
Sing. Talk to your father. Run.

Chapter 11

THE morning's classes were a nuisance because I just wanted to get to English and get the trial started. I had passed Ms. Stine in the hallway before homeroom, and she said she was looking forward to our presentations today. So, I figured that we all had the trial on our minds. It was intriguing to me that Ms. Stine was also wearing black pants and a purple sweater. Hers was a lavender cardigan over a creamy camisole with various shades of purple flowers washed over it. I've always been curious why we dress similarly sometimes for no apparent reason. Especially when it came to wearing purple. In fact, Austin had on a long-sleeved shirt, striped with shades of purple worn open over a black tee shirt and jeans. He commented on our similar outfits as we got our papers out and began helping to move the desks in the classroom around to arrange a mock courtroom.

Ms. Stine had shown us pieces of the film, *To Kill A Mockingbird*, rather than the whole thing, to help us picture the setting and get to know its characters. We didn't watch the court scene when the prosecutor puts on trial Tom Robinson, a black man in this Southern town around 1960. Accused of attacking a white woman, the defense brings up details about her injuries and about the crime that lead us to believe that the woman's father had actually beaten her when he saw her with the black man. So,

Austin and I are going to try to convince our jury, our modern jury, that he was not guilty.

We listened as the students assigned to the other team of lawyers presented the details of the case in their opening statement. Ms. Stine nodded at me as a sign that it was our turn. I stood up with my notes and grabbed as much volume for my voice from a deep breath as I could.

"We are here today to show the judge and jury that this innocent man," I pointed to the student representing Tom Robinson, "has been wrongly accused of a crime. He has been accused not because he has a history clean from unlawful behavior or even because he was in the wrong place at the wrong time. Those are reasons he is innocent. He has been wrongly accused because of our pre-judgment, our prejudice. Do you admit that you yourself have pre-judged others?" I looked up at no one in particular with my rhetorical question. "Maybe it was how the individual looked, not just his skin color or the shape of her eyes, but her clothes. Maybe it was what math class he was in or what he brought for lunch? Maybe it was even a rumor you heard that you never proved true? We are the guilty ones here. Not him. We will show today that Tom Robinson is not guilty of anything but showing compassion for another human being and being punished for it." I paused to look up again at the class. Everyone was looking at me, and I thought they understood by the transparent sunny yellow misting around them. I repeated, "We are the guilty ones here. Not him." I remained standing for an extra moment as the adrenaline subsided, and I was satisfied that I had spoken clearly and crisply. I didn't look up from my notes as much as I had planned to, but for our introduction, I thought we started off with an intellectual approach and conviction.

Then it was time for witnesses to start being called for questioning. Austin was going to handle this part as it required a little more spontaneous thinking and responding on the spot. The list of witnesses included the Sheriff; the father of the victim, Mr. Ewell; and the young woman herself, Mayella. We wouldn't get through anyone except the Sheriff on this first day, which was enough. It was difficult to keep all of the facts straight from the story and manage to appeal to our attitudes today. I thought Austin did a great job living up to the clever performance of the lawyer called Atticus Finch. Although Austin would never admit that he had a talent for the stage, some of his success on the athletic field is probably due to his ease in front of others. It's not hard for him to conceal himself behind a front that was barely discernible, or at least it doesn't seem to be.

Using up the mental energy that we did in English class worked up my appetite. Austin and I chatted about our case as we walked to the cafeteria for lunch. He couldn't hide the feeling of accomplishment he had, even though he wouldn't say himself that he thought he did a good job. His eyes sparked with gold that followed us through the hall of students walking to their own destinations undeterred by the colors I saw. It was uplifting to see his energy.

My high was depressed somewhat because I had to buy lunch again today to eat in the confines of the office. Only two more days of lunch detention. I guess this is why it's called a punishment, I admitted to myself. I kept my mind on the evening to come as I got in line and talked with Mindy for a few minutes before we had to part ways for the lunch period. We found ourselves discussing what we were going to have for dinner at the food court at the mall while we were still choosing our lunch items. It reminded me of the times that Mom would say that my eyes were bigger than my stomach; that was hard to understand at first for a little kid. Mom always had a lot of sayings that didn't always make sense to me immediately after she said them. It was one thing to hear it and quite another to have actually experienced it.

Finally the dismissal bell was ringing, and I was rushing as fast as I could to my locker to meet up with Mindy. I waited at her locker, pulled on my coat and balanced my backpack between my feet so that we could leave the school building together. Just as Austin and I had chatted at a heightened pace after our trial portion today, Mindy and I talked a lot, although I can't recall much of the conversation from then on during the bus ride home. When we arrived at her house, her mother was ready to take us to the mall, so we didn't waste any time leaving our backpacks in the front hall and getting into her mother's car.

I wasn't shopping for anything specific while Mindy was set on scoring an outfit, and probably Austin's company too, for New Year's Eve. I shared with Mindy the meeting that I had set up with Breck, so that was at the forefront of my anticipation. My stomach was definitely battling with butterflies inside, but I wasn't disturbed by its unsettled state. I tried to ignore it as we walked around stopping at the stores that we like to shop in the most. While Mindy was trying on a pair of jeans with brand new holes torn in them and an off-the-shoulder top in a soft brown, the color of a Golden Retriever, I was looking in the mirror next to the dressing rooms considering different pairs of earrings next to my ears still clasped to their plastic holders. Mindy's mom approved of the outfit when Mindy modeled it, so they purchased it, and I chose a pair of earrings for my pierced ears that dangled an emerald-cut amethyst surrounded by tiny glass chips from a small silver hoop. They looked like diamonds combined with the unusual square cut of the amethyst—the color would match my violet necklace. I felt like they were made for me. I kept them wrapped in the tissue paper and small bag and put them in my handbag to wear later to Winter Solstice.

We made a stop at the bath and body store to sample the lotions and matching scents while Mindy's mom mulled over a few different bath sets for gifts for the upcoming holidays. From this store I could see the flower shop where my mother worked part time; it was across the walkway diagonally closer to the food court. I expected that neither Mindy nor her mother would need to stop in there for any reason, but I wanted to go in. Just to see the colors and smell the fragrance and feel the humid coolness of the air in there that keeps the flowers fresh and alive.

I wanted to check the time on my phone, and as I dug under the wrapped earrings in my handbag, I realized I must've left it in in the front pocket of my backpack at Mindy's. I asked Mindy, who was searching for just the right orangey-red shade of nail polish. When she said it was just barely past five o'clock, I had plenty of time to stop in the flower shop before we headed towards the food court for dinner and to meet up with Breck at six. I told Mindy and her mother where I was going and that they could find me there if I hadn't returned to the bath and body store by the time they were ready to leave. I looked both ways as I crossed the walkway as if I were crossing the street. I could tell that the crowds had grown thicker due to the time of day and the time of year, but with no trouble I walked between people and into the flower shop. That's what it's called too, The Flower Shoppe, with the fancy spelling that looks like it should be written in curly calligraphy even though it isn't. I didn't recognize the man behind the counter at the register, but I did know the manager who was in the glass-encased walk-in refrigerator that lined the whole left wall of the store from front to back. I waved at her, and she put her hands over her mouth and opened her eyes wide when she saw me. I hadn't taken into account how she must be missing Mom, too.

"Oh, Violet," she ran towards me with her arms open for a hug. "How are you? It's so nice to see you." She grasped me firmly in her arms and then fidgeted with her hands as she took a step back to look at me with a tearful smile.

"I'm fine, thanks. How are you, Kathy?" It was always a little awkward, but she insisted that I call her by her first name. She said she felt old when people called her Mrs.

"Good, good." She nodded her head as she was trying to decide whether she believed it herself. "No, we're good, really. Business is good." I felt like she didn't want to bring up Mom after all this time, but that she couldn't help but think of her when she saw me. "How's your dad doing?" she continued, still fidgeting with her hands, smoothing her apron.

"He's fine. I'll tell him you asked," I said politely. Not knowing what else to say, I glanced into the walk-in cooler at all the fresh flowers stacked in various colors and sizes of vases as well as the larger white plastic containers holding cut flowers waiting for arrangements. The colors here don't overwhelm me even though there are so many and they're so natural and vivid. I think it's because they aren't emanating human energy; they are just colors existing in nature and are what they are. There isn't any intention behind the color I see. In fact, I'm very at ease here among the flowers' colors and scents.

"Come inside, Violet," Kathy said leading me over, seemingly glad that I gave us a way to change the course of our conversation. She showed me some of the newest arrangements she had for the holidays and talked about the flowers as if they were her very own pets. I could easily tell how much she adored the object of her job. She has the flowers organized by color, so it looked like a rainbow of flowers around me from traditional red roses to the violets I so loved.

A customer had walked into the store, so Kathy excused herself and left me to reflect on the flowers alone. I walked around to the smaller containers of purple flowers, many of which I didn't know by name. I looked closely at an arrangement in a white porcelain vase labeled purple lisianthus, which was a beautiful rose-like flower in a shade of purple straight from the crayon box. I bent down to smell them and saw that the vase was sitting on a small sturdy box with my name written on the top. The vase covered some of the letters, but it was definitely my name with a capital V, and I was becoming more certain that it was my mother's hand-writing etched in black ink on the silver lid. I narrowed my eyes not sure whether to believe what I was seeing. I carefully lifted the vase with two hands. I moved my head closer to the box trying to clear my eyes by opening them wider. I was in disbelief.

I looked around for a place to set the delicate vase, and I found a spot next to the tall metal cylinders of blue delphinium, the slim stiff stems laced with flowers up and down like a blue corn cob.

The silver box had a latch on the front, but it wasn't locked. I felt oddly guilty wanting to open it. That feeling in my stomach returned. I even turned my back towards Kathy and her customer as I gently lifted the lid. When I saw what was inside, I knew I had to take the box with me. It would fit in my handbag; it was about the size of a DVD case but about 3 inches thick. I debated about telling Kathy, afraid she wouldn't let me have it. I put it in my bag. I don't know why I kept it from her, but I was sure it was the right decision at the time. I quickly left the shop; Kathy was at the back of the store at the counter with the customer she had helped. Without even seeing them, I bumped right into Mindy as she and her mother were coming across the walkway for me.

"Ready to eat?" Mindy asked.

More jolts were stabbing my stomach, but I couldn't go back. I put on the truest smile I could and nodded, zipping up my handbag and protecting it under my arm.

We walked towards the food court, although food was furthest from my mind. Mindy talked above the din, but I wasn't really listening. This was too important. In my heart I knew I had made the right decision, and it couldn't get me in any trouble. The box was untraceable. No one would miss it. I hugged it closer, for it was meant to be mine.

Holly, with its berries and pointed green leaves, bordered this piece of paper probably torn from a pad. It curled up on one edge.

My Little Violet,
Eat chocolate-covered strawberries. They are divine. Treat
yourself at least once a day. Do the same for someone else.

Chapter 12

I still felt bad about leaving the flower shop the way that I had. I don't know why I acted the way I did. There was no reason for me to leave without asking permission to take the silver box with me. It had my name on it, after all. I didn't want Kathy to say no, and I didn't want to defy her. I was afraid I had made a mistake that would ripple into consequences I couldn't foresee. That worried me, but I brushed my violet quickly by my lips to inhale its calmness for a brief moment. It was done, and I couldn't go back.

Now there was nothing more to do but to act interested in dinner and return to the present. Hopefully, Breck was going to be meeting up with me soon, and I didn't want to be distracted and acting like a jerk. While we were eating our Asian dishes we chose from the array of restaurant kiosks, I realized that Breck was supposed to send me a text, just as he had said he would, to see when and where to meet up with us. I could feel my violet's glow burn red at its edges. I was mad at myself for carelessly leaving my phone back at Mindy's. I didn't know his number by heart to send him a message from Mindy's phone, so now he was going to think that I was standing him up or ignoring him. I felt so helpless and that I had ruined a good thing before it even started.

I played with the rice and vegetables on my plate and kept looking around for any sign of Breck. I was really hoping he'd show up in spite of my forgetfulness. Mindy's mom was talking on her phone across from us at the table, and Mindy was centered on finding Austin at the mall. I finally was able to start listening to her despite the other issues I felt were more important. As if Mindy's thoughts had come true, Austin came out of the game arcade with a couple of the football players. Mindy swatted my leg under the table with the backside of her hand.

"What should I do? What should I do?" Mindy didn't act like a giddy school girl much, so I knew how Austin flustered her when she acted this way.

"I'll get his attention, ok?" I started waving my arm above Mindy's head in Austin's direction.

Then she swatted my arm hard. "Violet, what are you doing?"

I started laughing. "I thought you wanted to talk to him." At least this was some comic relief. I was glad I could have a little fun. "What do you want me to do?" I tried to be serious.

As we were whispering, Austin and his friends made their way nearby our table anyway on their path to the pizza counter.

"Hey, Violet," Austin said in greeting as he walked by. He didn't really stop his stride, but I saw him look at Mindy and nod, the boys' version of a cool hello.

Mindy swatted my leg yet again, which I knew meant that I should engage him in some sort of conversation. She glared at me with gritted teeth.

"Uh, hey, Austin, what are you guys up to?" The words came out in pieces.

He stopped while the other boys continued in the direction of the pizza. "Just getting some pizza before Winter Solstice. When are you going over?" He gestured towards Mindy's mom as he could tell that she was our transportation and probably in charge.

"Well, I'm supposed to meet a friend at six, so we'll probably go over after that." Mindy nudged my knee with her knee trying to be stealthy with her interest. "And you?" I asked with exaggerated interest in my voice.

Austin grabbed ahold of the back of the chair next to Mindy's mom, right across from Mindy whose eyes were glued to his answer. "One of the guys has an older brother who's hanging out in the arcade with his buddy." He gestured behind him to the arcade and let go of the chair. It rocked back and forth with a little click on the tile floor. "We're getting a ride over with them after we eat. So we'll see you there."

Just as Austin was giving us the information Mindy so desperately wanted to hear, I saw Alexis strolling by the food court toward the game arcade with Brittany, the girl with whom Austin had ended his relationship recently. Austin's back was to them as he walked away towards his friends and the pizza, but in clear view of these girls to see the attention Austin had given us.

I saw bull's eye red shoot skyward from the girls as their eyes darted towards us, and suddenly my violet strangled my neck. I couldn't catch my breath; it happened so fast, I can't believe I didn't see it coming.

The accusations of "boyfriend-stealer" and other words that intimated a similar notion but were much more offensive were hurled towards us. Mindy's mother stood up while still on the phone and found herself in the middle of a screaming match, because her daughter was not standing quiet for these foul names being shot at her. Mindy's mom searched frantically around the area for security, holding the phone to her ear and giving commentary on the events.

The first words that came from my mouth were that we hadn't done anything, expecting that this logic would make Alexis and Brittany give up and walk away from this fight they had started. Mindy latched on to my idea and raised her voice, leaning on to the table holding our trays of food, but allowing the table to serve as a barrier. I wished it were a shield.

143

And in that moment, before I realized that the thought had materialized, Breck appeared in the food court accompanied by Clay. They must've been drawn to the yelling rather than the fact that their friends were involved. I saw Austin and his friends stunned at the spectacle, and his golden halo that he usually held high was flaking away in bits of confusion and embarrassment coated in blues and greens.

This was a mistake. I felt it in my gut. I couldn't see it all; the visions weren't making sense to me. My violet suffocated me with red—danger was immediate and tearing my insides out. The pain in my core was more troubling than it hurt. It would be devastating for us all. I didn't even know how seriously just yet.

The words rose in me like a recording, and I couldn't stop them. "She has been wrongly accused of a crime. She has been accused not because she has a history clean from unlawful behavior or even because she was in the wrong place at the wrong time. Those are reasons she is innocent. She has been wrongly accused because of your pre-judgment, your prejudice. Do you admit that you yourself have pre-judged others?" I looked up to see Austin's confusion grow on his face; he had heard these words before, but he still didn't come forward to help. "Maybe it was even a rumor you heard that you never proved true? You are the guilty ones here. Not her." My voice didn't sound like my own as the rushing of air into my throat roared in my ears. "We have let you bully us, and we won't let you kill us with it."

This wasn't right. These words weren't supposed to come out of my mouth. It was a song. It should've been music. But I couldn't see the notes on the page. The red page. The one from the book. Where was it? It was too hazy and too late. It was lost somewhere in my head with all the other colors.

Security guards were running up through the crowd that was gathering when I heard her say, "Just once more is all it will take."

I expected that the guards were the ones who had pushed

through and were carrying me away. But it was Clay and Breck who had stepped in to our defense. One of the guards stood around our table, and two others ushered Alexis and Brittany away from the food court. The guards threatened calling the police if we didn't clear the area.

We were suddenly out in the cold December air in the parking lot with Breck and Clay. I came to my senses. I was so grateful that Mindy's mother had grabbed my handbag along with Mindy's things from the table that I almost dropped to my knees right there next to the car. She put our bags into the trunk. Breck and Clay helped me into the back seat and sat on either sides of me as if they were still protecting me; Mindy sat in the front with her mother. No one said a word. I barely heard our breathing return to normal but easily saw the dark and violent red swirls around us begin to slow down to dust and become part of the air. It was hard for me to listen to separate thoughts because each of us was healing in different ways as we had different roles in the last encounter. I was relieved that my hasty wish didn't have more devastating consequences. My violet wasn't turning any shades of purple to show that I had resolved any conflict. The red veins in the purple-black petals twinkled through the array of colors I saw around us, almost like Christmas tree lights.

Clay, with his omnipresent humor from *The Pink Panther* and dubious French accent, said, "What? What did you say?"

We all started giggling yet we said nothing, not one of us. We appreciated his attempt at lightening up the situation. Mindy's mom laughed harder and answered him, "Nothing."

"You mean, you didn't just say: Stop the car, dear God, I beg of you, stop the car?" Clay himself laughed at his own rendition of the Inspector's lines, especially funny since we weren't even moving. I wasn't familiar with lines from the movie; nevertheless, Clay helped brighten our spirits with his words that spread like white clouds before me.

Mindy's mom said that she'd take us to Winter Solstice if we still wanted to go, and we all agreed that we would. We promised to stick together and to stay out of trouble. I was able to apologize to Breck for not having my phone to be able to make our "date," so to speak, and I thanked him for being there anyway. Clay entertained Mindy's mom with his talented accent, and I could tell that Mindy was enjoying his company as well, considering Austin hadn't come to our rescue. It gnawed at me that Austin was at the center of this confrontation, and yet he left an unscathed bystander. I pushed the thought down into my belly where most of the unresolved issues sit in my body, and I paid attention to the fact that Breck was here with me and was exceeding my expectations so far. I wondered what he saw in me at that moment but was a little afraid to try to listen.

The high school wasn't far from the mall, and the lights from the parking lot created an eerie luminosity from the road as we approached. It was barely dusk, but headlights shone from myriad directions under the cones of white light streaming from the light poles. Mindy's mom expertly found a spot without too much searching, and we had a short walk to the doors of the school. We left our bags and winter jackets in the car, in spite of Mindy's mom's urging that we take our coats. It's always so hot in the auditorium and cafeteria where most of the festivities are located, so we just had to make our way in and out of the building in the December temperature. It would probably be colder later on, but we agreed that we'd tough it out.

We left the anxiety and worry of meeting up with Alexis behind and walked in as a group in as high spirits as everyone else who was heading to the front steps of the school. I didn't see anyone I knew as we opened the lobby doors and freed the Christmas music into the night. One of the high school band ensembles must have been playing from inside the auditorium as people gathered at the snack stand for hot drinks and lined up to get into the school store. It's too small to allow more than a few students in at a time, but people were chatting in pairs waiting to get in. Everyone was mixing colors of calmness, which helped me to control my instinct to avoid the crowds that I feared. Breck was by my side, and that also gave me courage. Clay, Mindy and her mother separated from us almost immediately as we each were greeted by residents of the school district whom we all knew in different ways. I saw elementary school kids that I had babysat for in the neighborhood; Mindy started talking to her former field hockey coach from sixth grade; Mindy's mom went to get a cup of coffee and stood near the back of the auditorium to listen to the music. Clay continued through the lobby to the cafeteria where a variety of stations were set up with activities and presentations from the schools celebrating different holidays. Breck wanted to get something to drink first, and then we decided to try to find Clay and make our way to the chorus stage.

I thought I was already too late for our performance, which was fine with me after the way the evening had taken an unpleasant turn. I wasn't in the mood to sing, and I really wanted to just spend some time with my friends, especially Breck. He was turning out to be such a respectable friend, considering I hadn't really treated him very well so far. What was wrong with me? I wouldn't be surprised if my friends all turned on me. I seemed so twisted inside out, unable to do the right thing. It always used to be so easy. I didn't understand what was happening. Did life all of a sudden become that much more difficult in eighth grade?

At least I was grateful that Breck had befriended Clay, or even if it were the other way around. I always thought that I was a good judge of character, and Clay was as good as any character I've ever met. Smart and funny, too, in an inoffensive, unobtrusive way. On the other hand, I had always admired Austin and his golden essence, but he let me down. I wasn't sure what to think.

Breck bought himself a hot chocolate and a bottle of water

for me, and we stayed close as we weaved our way through the mixture of students and adults, from little elementary schoolers being led by tight hands of their parents to graduates who long to return from college on their winter breaks to see former teachers and old friends. The music changed from rhythmic, familiar carols to melodic folk tunes sailing around the lobby decorated for the Winter Solstice—the moon, snowflakes and snowmen, tinsel in our school colors of navy blue, silver and white. I was thinking about Dad just then, because we were beginning to relax. I wanted to share something fun with him. It had been too long in between fun times with us.

I found the chorus director in time to join the eighth grade chorus sing the two pieces we had prepared for tonight, a joyous Christmas piece and a traditional Hanukkah song. I was able to focus on the music. Breck tried to pretend he wasn't staring at me the entire time, but I knew he was even with the spot lights making it hard to see in the crowd.

When our group finished, I thanked the director and parted ways with some of the other singers. We saw Ms. Stine leaning with her back on the farthest wall from the stands in the cafeteria holding a Styrofoam cup with both hands. She had been watching our performances and appeared to be waiting for the next group to take the stage. I specifically walked over to introduce Breck to her. She seemed to approve of him with a polite greeting, which made me feel pleased. We stood by and listened till the end of the song and continued to walk around enjoying the sights and sounds of the holiday. Clay was sitting on top of a booth near the back of the cafeteria where the windows reach floor to ceiling, as if he were guarding the scene. As much as the wall of windows let out the light and spirit of our evening, they let in the darkness just as easily. It made an unsettling contrast of colors for me, but I was still keeping any panic at bay. We stopped to talk to Clay and could observe the entire room just about from this vantage point. It was colorful and festive and daunting at the same time. It was as if I were tugging at the violet around my neck, ignoring its shrinking tightness and trying to just breathe through it like a mouse might snapped in a trap.

I let Clay and Breck exchange their boyish banter about sights in the room while I quietly endured my inner emotions. Finally, I couldn't ignore it any longer.

"Breck," I said, knowing the crease in my forehead was wrinkling visibly. "I'm not feeling too well." I knew I had to just admit to my phobia or else he'd assume I was trying to ditch our night together yet again. "Crowds sometimes don't, uh, don't, uh...well, they make me panic. Like I can't breathe." I was beginning to think it wasn't only just the crowd this time. There was something else there. I listened.

"Well, let's go outside and get some fresh air. Would that be okay?" Breck looked at Clay with the question instead of me, as if Clay were my brother or protector or something.

Clay answered nonchalantly, "Yeah, go right out here." He gestured with his thumb right behind him. The booth where he sat was adjacent to the double glass doors that led to the breezeway behind the school between the main building and the new addition which included a new gymnasium and natatorium.

Breck looked at me as if to ask permission, and I nodded and hooked my arm in his to walk right outside without any argument. I took a deep breath of the cold winter air, let go of Breck and put both of my hands on the back of the old wooden bench in the courtyard there before I lost my balance. I bent at my waist and took in few slow, deep breaths.

I knew right then that I should've listened to my dreams. I should've known better when I couldn't see the colors of Mindy when she vanished in my dream the other night.

"We have to find Mindy." I straightened up quickly and tried to catch my breath, even though I knew I was hyperventilating.

"Ok," Breck said, a little unsure. "Do you need to go home?"

"No, we just have to find her. I'm, uh, I think...." I tried to finish my sentence but was sliding the violet on its cord faster and faster without even knowing I was doing it. It was black, and I knew if I looked inside the cafeteria that I'd be able to spot the blackness of Alexis' evil somewhere among the people who were innocently surrounding her with their joy. Breck hesitantly took my arm, and we walked back in through the double doors. I squinted my eyes as the worry wrinkled my nose and forehead.

It was as if Clay expected us to come back inside. "A rumor is going around that Ms. Stine has a knife and plans to kill any of her students she sees," he said with seriousness and urgency, two traits that Clay doesn't possess usually. But I noticed some sapphire blue just barely rising off of Clay's body. I couldn't recall his usual colors, and he seemed doubtful of his own statement. But, at the same time, he was wasting no time preparing to leave.

People were starting to exhibit signs of distress, gathering friends and family members, whispering to each other and looking around suspiciously. I couldn't see Ms. Stine anywhere although she had just been waiting on the other side of the room enjoying the Winter Solstice like everyone else.

"Maybe we should just go right back out to the parking lot from this door," Breck said as he stepped back towards the door we just had come in.

I was confused, my panic starting to boil over. As the room started to spin in front of me, I saw Austin's face, Harley's face, Mindy's mom's face, stretching into horrid visions of bleeding eyes, ripping flesh and echoing, screaming throats. I tore at the violet around my neck and felt it tear off in my fist as I fought to get oxygen, to let the air back into my perishing body. Without my violet, I could save myself from seeing what I didn't want to see.

When I opened my eyes, I was lying there on the floor of the cafeteria next to Breck. He was lying unconscious beside me. I saw him breathing as if he were sleeping in his own bed. Clay wasn't there, and neither were Mindy or her mother. I sat up gingerly, propping my hands behind me and leaving my legs limp and resting straight out in front of me. One of my shoes was missing, but I saw it lying about a foot away near the group of police officers standing by the double glass doors who were talking to Cropsie, my neighbor.

As soon as I had questioned what he must've been doing here, I recalled seeing him dragging his Christmas wreath and tangled lights down the street not long ago. He always loved this time of year, so it was definitely a treat for him to attend Winter Solstice for some thriving holiday spirit. I needed to know why he was talking to the police, where my friends were, and whether Breck was going to be okay.

My stupid phone. Why did I forget my phone? I wanted to talk to my dad.

Storm-colored paper revealed the graphite script of simple pencil.

My Little Violet,
Things you've done and said may be forgotten by others,
but you must live with your memories the rest of your life.
Don't leave any regrets behind.

Chapter 13

THE cafeteria was quiet, but there were still people around. I didn't waste time identifying the adults I saw, but I sensed that the imminent danger had passed. The colors of the room were muted, although blackness still lingered. I was trying to focus on the green, like pine needles poking my skin, reminding me that I was alive and felt secure with Breck at least beside me. I shook him gently by the arm and said his name, hoping that would be all it took to awaken him. When he wouldn't stir, I steadied myself and slowly stood up to find help.

As much as I didn't want to bring Cropsie's attention upon myself, the police officers to whom he was talking were my closest aid. They stopped immediately to help me without my even having to ask.

One of the officers surprised me when he called me by name, "Violet, you and your friend here," he pointed to Breck, "can thank Mr. Cropsie here for keeping you out of harm's way."

I didn't know whether I should thank him or ask him whether he was sure that Breck was really okay. Plus, I was worried about Mindy and Clay.

"Of course. Thank you," I said. I faced Cropsie and tried to look at him in the eye. It's not that I didn't appreciate it. But, he seemed as uncomfortable with my graciousness towards him as

I felt being near him. "Is there someone here who can check on him?"

And with that, an emergency medical technician had been on his way over and knelt down right next to Breck. "We're getting around as fast as we can. All the serious cases are on their way by now." He moved with experience around Breck, checking his pulse and breathing, his pupils. "He should probably get a head scan just to be safe, but his breathing is fine. I suspect he hit his head in a fall."

Relieved that Breck was going to be fine, I stuttered the question stuck in my throat. "What...uh...what serious cases?" I asked, wondering if I would hear something I dreaded.

"Mostly people who were pushed down and trampled by the crowds trying to escape the building," he said as he was looking for something in a kit. "Only the one was stabbed."

"Do you know who it was? Or who did it?" Again I asked, unsure whether I wanted the truth. Did he really say stabbed?

The EMT must have given Breck something like smelling salts, because he didn't answer me and told Breck to stay still. He gently put his hand behind Breck's head.

"Yeah, it feels like you've got a golf ball back here, son. Is it sore?" The EMT screwed his face up with sympathy. Breck didn't answer. He was still trying to open his eyes and make sense of where he was; at least that was what it seemed like to me. With a positive spark in his voice, he continued, "The thing is, better the golf ball on the outside than the inside. Know what I mean?" He explained to me the fact that it was good that the swelling was on the outside of Breck's skull. It meant that his body was handling the injury, but he should probably get it checked out as soon as he could. I was relieved but still didn't have all the information about what had happened here tonight.

My phone was at Mindy's, and my stuff was in her mom's car. And as I looked around the cafeteria, the two of them weren't to be found. There were a few people standing in groups, talking quietly, arms around each other, shaking their heads, probably confused like I felt. I criss-crossed my legs and sat up straighter.

Dad was out of town, so I didn't want to worry him. I am resilient, I told myself. I knew I'd be sturdy on my feet. I had control and a clear head, and I just had to make a decision about what to do to get us out of here.

Breck was starting to come back to himself. He sat up and crossed his legs in front of him, a copy of me, and rested his elbows on his knees. He looked at me, straight in the eyes, and said, "You don't remember what happened, do you?" He said it like a statement, not a question. He knew the answer, and he also knew he was the only one here who could tell me what occurred. I was more afraid of the answer than I had been when I was just imagining the worst. His even tone coated the curve of his shoulders, which scared me because it was so different from his usual posture.

Breck lifted his chin and scanned the cafeteria. When he saw Cropsie still talking to the police officers, he stood up without a word to me, although he let me help him gain his balance.

With an outstretched hand, Breck interjected politely, "Excuse me, sir. Thank you for helping my friends." He shook Crospie's hand with firmness. Cropsie waved his left hand as if to say it was nothing; he looked as if he was going to say something, and then he changed his mind. He never was known to say much. A man of action, not words, I guess. I studied him more than I ever had before, and I berated myself during the moments that Breck thanked him for having pre-judged Cropsie myself. Seeing him in the neighborhood, I thought he was walking around aimlessly. I never thought he was a man of any substance, any intelligence even, certainly not someone who would do something kind for someone else. Obviously, that's what he did, and I would have never expected it. It reminded me of something I knew, yet couldn't place.

Breck arranged with one of the police officers to give us a ride, once we decided where to go. No one was at my house, so that didn't make any sense; plus, I didn't have my key or phone. Breck told the officer to take us to Breck's house, and that's when he explained to me what had happened. We rode in the darkness and chill of the December night, but I didn't shiver from the cold.

Mindy was dead. No melon. No colors. Just like in my dream. Once Clay had heard the rumor that was rushing around the school that Ms. Stine was planning to kill her students, panic had already set in. Parents were grabbing their little children and leaving first. Friends of ours and other middle school students who had been dropped off and didn't have rides began to scatter while trying to text and call for their parents to pick them up. The lobby, the auditorium, and the cafeteria became a heated battlefield. Those who were trying to make phone calls were being shoved aside. Fear changed people's colors from their usual essence: I've seen them turn an ugly dark yellow with mistrust or the sea blue of perseverance and patience. As Breck shared the story, I had glimmers of seeing a shining black blanket, dark and thick like the fresh tar spread on the road. I remembered. I felt weak in its evil grasp.

Breck said that he had seen the girls he recalled from the mall approaching the exit where Clay, Breck and I had been gathered at the back of the cafeteria. They seemed intent on getting outside, but he didn't think they seemed panicked as most others appeared to be.

"I never saw Mindy," he said, sounding helpless about it. His shoulders and head drooped as we sat in the back seat of the police car. "Clay went to find her once he knew that I was with you. He made me promise not to let you out of my sight. Once those girls passed us and left out those back doors, you had passed out. I tried to pull you out of the way so that we wouldn't get stepped on. I guess that's when I must've hit my head." He rubbed the bump as he thought about it.

"So, how do you know that Mindy's...," I didn't want to say it. "How do you know?" I asked the question louder in frustration, not anger. I could feel tears filling my eyes, and I instinctually reached for my violet around my neck to calm myself. It wasn't there.

Breck saw me grasp my neck in shock, and he reached into his pants pocket. He handed me my violet on its cord. The clasp was broken. "You tore it off your neck. You seemed like it was strangling you, like you couldn't breathe."

I was so grateful that I hadn't lost it. I thanked him and held it up to my mouth in cupped hands. I inhaled deeply while Breck continued. As lost as I felt, my violet was just violet. Like a fresh bruise.

"All I know is people were saying that Mindy was stabbed. I'm not sure who said it or how they knew it was her. By that time, the police and...and everything," he threw up his hands not being able to finish his words. Breck leaned back in the seat and let me lean against him under his arm. I felt him kiss me on top of my head almost like Dad does. It made me need to talk to Dad, but again, that would have to wait. I had a lot to tell him. I kissed my violet and stuffed it in the pocket of my jeans for now.

We rode in the darkness in each other's comforting grasp, but my mind couldn't stay quiet.

"So, it must've been Alexis, right? She and Brittany must've followed us from the mall knowing we'd be at Winter Solstice." I was thinking aloud. "The police have to know that, right?" I wanted affirmation of the obvious. We were in a police car after all, but the officer didn't say anything.

"But what about that teacher you introduced me to, Ms. Stine? She was the one that was supposed to be the threat. She had a knife," Breck said this as if it were a definite fact.

I released myself from Breck's arm and looked him in the face. "I know she didn't do this. Alexis was after Ms. Stine just like she was after Mindy. Somebody had a knife, but it wasn't Ms. Stine. It couldn't have been." I thought for a minute and composed myself. This was complicated, and right now there wasn't the time to straighten it all out. We were pulling up to Breck's house. The porch light was on, and we could see Breck's dad's face in the window stoic on top of his broad shoulders. He disappeared from our view and was opening the front door and descending the steps immediately. Breck's mother was already skipping a few steps ahead of him.

He approached the car and started speaking with the officer while Breck and I waited to be released from the back seat of the police car. I hadn't thought about it before now; the handles don't open the doors from the inside. Finally, the officer, walking around to the sidewalk to talk directly to Breck's father, opened the back door on the passenger side. We slid across the back seat to get out. Breck's parents hugged him tightly, and his mother didn't let him go until he said in her ear that he wanted to introduce me to them, which he did.

I tried to be as polite as I could. My little hello didn't sound like my own. His mother was quite attractive, with a slim and athletic build, even with hair pulled back in a ponytail and a faded gray Penn State sweatshirt over leggings and puffy white slippers. After she gave me a hug, too, she crossed her arms and bounced on her toes to try to warm up in the dry cold of the night air.

I wanted to talk to the police officer and make sure that he had the whole story as to what had gone on prior to this whole incident including the argument at the mall. I wanted them to know that this was based on rumor not fact, that they couldn't blame anyone but Alexis. But, I wasn't given the opportunity. When I tried to talk to the officer before he left us there on the sidewalk, he said that I should call the police station to speak to an investigator tomorrow, that is, if someone doesn't contact us first for our stories.

I was frustrated, but we still didn't have any firsthand

information from Mindy's mother or Clay. I wanted to go to the hospital, but Breck's father insisted that we come inside and rest. His mother was already making hot chocolate and had laid out an tray of cookies that looked like the misfits from her Christmas cookie batches. I hadn't realized that I needed something to eat, but the green and red sugar crystals made my mouth water seeing them sparkle on top of sugar cookies that were broken or had lost an edge to the spatula or oven. We sat at the kitchen table and ate while Breck filled in his parents on the night's events. I was surprised they weren't annoyed with me for putting Breck in harm's way on our first "date" no less. But they were very pleasant and expressed their relief that we were all right. Breck's dad agreed to call the hospital in the morning to check on Mindy and Clay, but his mother wanted to take him right away to get a scan for the bump on his head. She apparently was very persuasive, because shortly after we had finished our snack, she came downstairs in a pair of jeans and sneakers, still in her sweatshirt, and Breck's dad had also changed his clothes. As tired as I was, I was glad that we'd be going to the hospital. I needed to talk to Clay, to Mindy's mother, to Mindy, if I could. I wasn't going to let myself believe that she was gone. I stuffed my hand in my pocket just to touch my violet. It didn't reassure me like I wanted it to.

"Here," Breck held out his hand. "Give it to me. I'll fix the clasp."

I hesitantly handed him my necklace. Of course I trusted him. He had saved it for me the whole time I was unconscious. He went right to a drawer in the kitchen and pulled out a pair of pliers, a small pair. He held the clasp with one hand and bent the metal back into a curved crescent, like the moon, so that the other end with its teardrop could be hooked inside it. His handiwork didn't take more than a few seconds. He replaced the pliers in the drawer, shoved it closed with his hip, and handed me my necklace back as if it were no feat whatsoever.

"Breck," I said, "I'm not sure that I thanked you yet tonight. So, thank you. Again." I smiled and felt a twinge in my stomach. I wanted to give him a kiss. Not a romantic kiss necessarily, but a thank you kiss. Because the words just didn't feel like enough. But Breck's parents were right there, getting coats and a couple of bottles of water and locating car keys. Instead, I asked him to clasp my violet back in place around my neck. I turned back around to face him and held his hands in mine for an extra few moments. "Thank you," I repeated, not embarrassed that he could see the blush spread across my cheeks.

The four of us got into Breck's dad's car and drove over to the hospital. Hopefully the wait in the emergency room wouldn't be too long for Breck to have his head checked over; but I was more interested in the information that was waiting there for us. Whether I liked it or not. Breck lived closer to the hospital than I did. Harrisburg Hospital is set right on the banks of the Susquehanna River, which gives it this appearance of solace and peace, because lights from the bridges and the moonlight shimmer on the dark, tranquil water. Even the traffic that circles around the buildings is muted and calm. I was afraid I would not find the news at the hospital to be as reassuring as the scene I saw around it. It was already was turning out to be a long night for a Wednesday.

A shiny brand new sheet of paper glowed like a city skyline silhouette at night. I can't quite name the color, somewhere between gray and beige and yellow, but I knew the handwriting on the back.

My Little Violet,
Quite simply, we all learn that life isn't fair. The rest isn't
all that simple.

Chapter 14

BRECK'S mom stood in line waiting to check in while Breck's dad sat in one of the plastic chairs in the waiting room of the emergency area of the hospital next to Breck and me. Unfortunately, there were a few others from school also waiting with their parents for a variety of injuries. I didn't know them, but I recognized the navy blue school jackets and faces of some of them. The television mounted in the corner showed CNN, and I kept glancing up at it even though I had no interest in the stories being broadcast. The scroll at the bottom of the screen antagonized me. I was afraid there would be more secrets revealed, and I didn't think I could stand anything more. The time displayed a few minutes before three in the morning. I almost felt a twang of joy out of habit realizing that none of us would probably be going to school today, but the reality of sitting in the hospital pushed that away immediately.

Breck's mom stuck her wallet back in her handbag and sat on the end of the row of chairs next to Breck's dad, farthest from me. She whispered to him. I wondered if she had found out any information about Mindy, but I hated to be the one who kept asking. With all these people here from school, didn't anyone know anything? Why wasn't anyone talking about what happened? Then, it occurred to me. I was Mindy's best friend, so maybe everyone was trying to spare my feelings by not talking about it. I couldn't wait any longer. Just as I had decided to ask Breck's mom, a nurse called on Breck to go back to a bed to be seen by a doctor.

"Breck Stewart." Breck's mom rose from her chair. She waited for Breck to go first.

I noticed a slight hesitation as his mom made eye contact with his father. "No, go ahead. You all go back. That's what you'd do if I weren't here. I'll be fine," I said. "I am fine," I corrected. They looked at each other trying to decide. I was sliding my violet up and down its cord, as usual, a cue to my nervousness. It was frustrating not to be able to decipher the past, having little recollection except for my visions, while also being unclear on the present.

Breck's dad said to his wife, "I'll stay with Violet. Just have a nurse come out to get me if you need me. We'll wait right here." He leaned over and patted me on my knee.

Breck squeezed my hand before dropping it in my lap as he left the waiting area. This was going to be torture just waiting. I had to find out something.

After what only ended up being about four minutes of watching CNN, I told Breck's dad that I was going to use the restroom. I was unsettled just sitting and waiting. My mind was preoccupied with my friends, but I couldn't help noticing the shades of blues and greens of sadness and healing swirling around the room and the hallway where I was headed towards the restroom. I passed the reception area where Breck's mom had checked in. Inside a row of window boxes sat the nurses as if they were going to hand out a bag of fast food if you paid accordingly. I found a nurses' station through the double doors separating the waiting room from the emergency room beds. Sitting there like a big round doughnut, baked brown around the circular sides and glazed on top with a white counter flecked with colored folders like paper sprinkles. Anything or anyone seated behind the counter was hidden by its tall height. I couldn't resist an attempt to get answers to the questions running over and over through my head.

I peered over the counter by stretching up on my toes, trying not to disturb the folders lying on top. Two nurses were chatting quietly, one typing while the other looked over her shoulder at the computer screen. The one not typing smiled at me.

"Excuse me. I'm...uh...looking for the restroom." I hoped to catch them off guard and be willing to share information with me about patients I wasn't related to. I figured that was how it was on TV shows.

The smiling nurse pointed to my right. "Right down there on your right."

"Thanks," I said and started in that direction. I stepped back to the doughnut desk. "I was wondering...uh...about some of the people that came here from the school...uh...incident. A friend of mine from my school. Two friends actually." The typing nurse stopped typing and looked at me along with the smiling one. "Mindy Allen and Clay Grant. From Cobalt Valley." They still looked at me, but the smile vanished into a sorrowful frown. I felt my heart starting to pound like it was popcorn popping.

The typing nurse was the one who replied, "Let's see what I can tell you." She seemed earnest in her computer search, but I waited with my hands folded on the counter. They were cold with nervousness. Or was it fear. The waves of blue around us seemed to swell. "A-l-l-e-n," she said matching her keystrokes. "I don't see anything here." I sighed not realizing I had been holding my breath. "No Clay Grant either. Sorry."

I thanked them wholeheartedly and walked down the corridor to the restroom. I pushed the door like it was a stone boulder blocking my way. With effort, it swung open. I turned the faucet to cold and splashed water on my face. My reflection in the mirror unnerved me. My eyes were bloodshot with exhaustion; my skin now blotched with roses where the cold water had stung my cheeks. I tried to comb my hair smooth with my fingers, letting a wave fall over my ear and then pushing it back behind it again.

I returned to the waiting room with no change to the confusion and loss I was feeling, and now Mr. Stewart was gone. I looked at the empty chairs trying to make sense of how long I could have been gone. Without another moment passing, I felt forced to seek answers myself. I rubbed my eyes and my face with the pads of my fingers. My cheeks and hands thawed in the warmth of the hospital's sterile corridors and in my renewed purpose. I couldn't go far, however. Doors between the emergency suite and other areas of the hospital were inaccessible; they were shut tight with small boxes requiring identification and access codes mounted on the walls. That feeling that rumbles in my stomach when I'm feeling trapped was scrambling around inside trying to get out. I took a deep breath of my violet and shrugged off toward the exit for some fresh air.

"Violet!"

"Dad!"

His arms around me felt like a fortress, so strong and impenetrable. Shielding me from the cold and the truth, I didn't want him to let go. When a good minute had passed, I released my grip. Clay had been standing next to Dad the entire time.

In his usual quick wit, Clay said, "What's a guy gotta do around here to get some love? I mean, I saved your life once already today."

I gave him a hug then, but I noticed that he hadn't spouted off any French accent or lines that the inspector might say.

"Clay? What happened, Clay?" The tears started coming now. I had been brave and hopeful long enough. I knew in my heart what he was going to say. I covered my ears, and Dad held me in his arms.

"Mindy died on the way to the hospital. She was stabbed from behind in her ribs. Bleeding into her lungs suffocated her." Clay could barely get out the words.

"Did you see her, Clay? Did you see her do it? Please say you did. Please say it," I was almost ranting, eyes closed, my limbs trembling.

He shook his head. "I saw Ms. Stine running from the cafeteria in her black coat. We had just been talking to her, and when I turned back around, she was already halfway to the exit to the parking lot at the opposite corner from where I had left you and Breck. Mindy was already...hurt," he said carefully.

"Not Ms. Stine, Clay. Alexis! Did you see Alexis?" My legs were weakening in frustration.

Dad interrupted, "Let's go get your things from Mindy's. We can talk this out later. You both need some rest."

There was no doubt I really wanted to get my things from Mindy's, but I couldn't just leave without making sure Breck was all right and that his parents knew where I was.

"Dad, I need you to meet Breck first. I wouldn't have made it if it weren't for him and Clay."

We entered the hospital right back through to the emergency area and into the waiting room. Breck's family was still not there, so to the doughnut desk we went. We were able to send a message back to them via the nurses as cell phones were impermissible in the hospital. Breck's dad came out quickly to intercept our departure.

My dad shook his hand firmly and gratefully, "Thank you for taking care of my daughter in my absence. I appreciate it more than you know."

"I know you'd do the same," Mr. Stewart nodded in fatherly understanding with Dad. With a brief exchange that they'd likely see each other in the neighborhood as Mr. Stewart was hoping to sell Mrs. Suden's house soon, Dad, Clay and I left the hospital.

The early morning sky held this beautiful rising sun behind cotton candy pink clouds sticking to the horizon. That was all I remembered as the ride home rocked me to sleep.

I woke up on the couch in our living room, behind the parlor, a small room where we didn't sit much anymore. But the cushions were deep and soft and made me wonder where I was when I opened my eyes. Lying on top of me was an old furry blanket that reminded me of what a zebra would look like if it were brown and in need of a bath. I kicked it off and sat up on the couch slowly. My head was feeling dizzy with lack of sleep and overwhelming worry. I leaned back on the couch and was able to see out the front window of the parlor. A light snow was falling steadily enough for me to see the downy flakes shimmering in the strong winter sunshine. It was definitely mid-day at least. I guessed I had probably slept a good seven hours or so since we had left the hospital. I shrugged off groggy heaviness and got up to look for Dad. I wondered whether we had stopped at Mindy's last night for my things. The thought of her stopped me cold. I fell to my knees right there in the parlor before I made it to the hallway and sobbed hard. Dad came running in and knelt on the floor right next to me.

"Vi, are you okay? Did you fall?" He pushed my hair back and kissed me on the top of my head, like he often does. It didn't comfort me like it usually did though. The sobs still hammered out of my throat, my gut. I didn't answer him. I just curled up right there on the cold floor and wished all this hurt would go away. I knew I wished it and it felt selfish. But I hoped it wasn't a waste.

We didn't have to go back to school today or tomorrow. Due to the tragedy at school, the loss of Mindy and the twenty or so others who had been injured in the panic, Winter Solstice ended and began our break on the same day. Clay and I went over to Mindy's around dinner time. Dad took us over bringing pizzas and a huge tossed salad from Pierro's. Dad had decided it was best to give Mindy's parents time alone last night after enduring the deep loss that must be breaking their hearts in pieces if it felt anything like mine. Other cars were lined up in front of Mindy's house. I guessed that grandparents and other close relatives were gathered in mourning.

I was frustrated with the fact that I needed to grieve and I wanted to help Mindy's parents find justice. So I wanted to deliver that to them. Not just dinner. I hadn't begged Dad yet to call the police about the investigation, but I had asked at least six or seven times. He assured me there would be an opportune time for the replay of events and my version of the truth. Even though Dad was not a litigating attorney who spent time in court presenting convincing arguments, he still played the role of logic and knew when my emotions were getting in the way. Like Atticus Finch's defense arguments in *To Kill A Mockingbird*, which, by the way, we hadn't really gotten to finish in English class. I'm guessing time will tell as to Ms. Stine's role in all of this. The knots twist up inside when I think that she might get mixed up in Alexis' devious plan. Or that she already was. That just doesn't make any sense to me.

We had to trudge through an inch of fresh wet snow up to Mindy's house with the food. A young woman with a pleasant hello and Mindy's tall slim build and fair freckled face opened the door.

"You must be Violet," she said before we could introduce ourselves. "Please," she stopped talking but opened the front door wide to allow us inside.

The conversations were in low voices but surprisingly upbeat. As I had guessed, it was Mindy's aunt, her mother's sister, who had greeted us and introduced us to a few relatives as she freed our hands of the salad and graciously thanked us on behalf of the family while Dad laid the pizza boxes on the counter next to a half-eaten coffee cake and a bowl of mixed fruit cut in cubes.

I didn't know what to say or what to do. I felt like I must seem rude and uncaring, but I just couldn't put words together. What was I supposed to say to make Mindy's parents feel better? No one's words could fill that empty feeling, the combination of hurt and anger and grief and wondering why.

Clay seemed like he instinctually knew what to say and do. He went right over to Mindy's parents to say he was sorry and that he would miss Mindy very much. I saw the pain in his eyes just then. They were round and glassy like deep water that has a bottom somewhere far below the surface. He had really liked Mindy a lot. I had forgotten until the honesty in his words to her parents. Dad poured Mindy's dad and himself a drink, and they walked into the living room to sit and talk with the other men sitting in there watching TV. In Clay's honorable fashion, he saved me again.

He waved me over to the table where he stood next to Mindy's mom. "Violet doesn't know what to say, Mrs. Allen, but we," he cleared his throat and continued with his French accent, "we will not stop till we solve zis crime." His try to lighten the mood made everyone at the table smile in good nature. He looked at me straight in the eye then, and said, "We promise." It was then that the smiles disappeared, and I think they all believed him. I did.

Mindy's mother made sure that I didn't forget my backpack and my handbag that I had taken to the mall. As anxious as I was to check through my things, I set them by the door so that I would not leave them behind by accident. Dad checked on us in the kitchen, but as more of our friends from school had begun to stop by, Clay and I suggested we stay for a while longer. So, Dad went back into the living room, and our group grew from the kitchen to the dining room. The day had already darkened into night and along with it, the low voices began to laugh loudly at times and stories about good times circled around friends. As the crowd began to thin, Breck showed up with his parents. His mother brought a box of hot coffee and doughnuts. She told Mindy's mother that the coffee was just as good warmed up for breakfast and this way she wouldn't have to make any when she woke up. I think Mindy's mom really appreciated it, although I didn't imagine her nights would be too restful for a while.

I was very glad to see Breck. We gave each other a playful bear hug hello, and he filled me in about his head injury. He was supposed to take it easy, but the scan found no serious trauma. Clay, Breck and I had talked to a lot of different people from school tonight, parents too. Clay spent some extra time with Mindy's little brother. Clay must have known that he liked to play games on Mindy's phone, because Clay handed him his to play with. Harley said she was sure she had seen Brittany at Winter Solstice, though she couldn't say she saw Alexis. The longer we talked, or as Clay would say investigated, the more I was convinced that we had to talk to the police in the morning. There was significant motive here, in my opinion, and if Ms. Stine and our reading of *To Kill A Mockingbird* was worth anything, I was not going to spare the truth here and let a bully prevail.

It was getting past nine o'clock, and Dad had to work in the morning downtown. Breck offered to take Clay home so that they could hang out till the Allens kicked them out or went to bed. I think the family was appreciating the diversion of so much company, especially with the time of year and all. We said our good-byes; Breck told me he'd call me tomorrow. Dad grabbed my backpack and slung it over his shoulder. I picked up my handbag carefully and felt the silver box bumping my side as I carried it to the car.

We put both bags in the backseat, but before I climbed in next to Dad in the front, I unzipped the pocket of my backpack to retrieve any missed messages on my phone. I even joked around with Dad about how long we were apart, although I know cell-phones can be replaced. Not like best friends.

I sat in the passenger seat next to Dad and rubbed my hands together trying to warm up in the cold car, having sat there all day in the light snowfall. He started the engine, turned on the defrost and got back out to scrape the windshield while I rebooted my phone by plugging it in to Dad's auto charger. Seven messages blinked at me dated yesterday while we were at the mall. I wasn't surprised at all at the sender. I showed Dad the earrings I had bought and never got to wear last night instead of showing him the messages on my phone first.

It was paper as thick and soft as toilet tissue. One side was washed in a bright orange. A green hill of wildflowers was painted in watercolors on the other side. Her handwriting stood out on the orange.

My Little Violet,
Secrets should be savored. But they can serve a purpose when shared with the right person at the right time.

Chapter 15

INSTEAD of going home to get some much needed rest as we intended to do, and despite the fact that Dad had to work tomorrow, I spent the next twenty minutes or so explaining the litany of events that Alexis had caused from the times she had interrupted our English class and seemed to treat Ms. Stine with rude coldness to the unintended drama between Mindy and Brittany to the confrontation witnessed by many bystanders at the mall. I remembered that I didn't even have to serve the last two days of lunch detention for the incident with Alexis in the cafeteria, as I was telling Dad what I thought had incited Alexis to target me with her nasty text messages.

We drove to the police station even though it was the second night in a row that we would be up late trying to make sense of these turns of events. It felt as if we no sooner had tried to understand and move past the shock, the despair, that I would have to stand up straight in the face of another unexpected blow, like I was a football player new to the line taking a shot in the gut because I didn't know what play was to come.

As relieved as I was that Dad was ready to help Mindy's case by taking me to the police station, I knew that I would have to repeat for the third time all of the attacks that Alexis had initiated. Reliving each of the moments as they flashed through my mind stirred a mixture of anger and frustration and grief at the loss of my best friend. I wasn't going to let Ms. Stine, or anyone else for that matter, be dragged into Alexis' vat of lies and hateful ways of treating others. When we walked into the police station that was dedicated to the neighborhoods that served our school district, I was pleasantly surprised by my surroundings but eerily had a foreboding feeling that I'd been here before. I denied any stray from my purpose here and now. I recalled that the building was no different from any other office building I had ever been in, although I've not been in many. A few intersecting hallways that were narrow and freshly painted eggshell spread out before us as we stood in the entryway facing a glass-enclosed reception desk. Dad explained who we were, displayed his driver's license when asked, and then put his arm around me and led me through a door that was unlocked from the other side.

A police officer, whom I didn't recognize from the night of the incident, politely greeted us and led us into a larger room that, again, looked like any ordinary office building. Desks were arranged in pods, similar to how we move our desks at school into groups of four or six. Their desks were in various stages of neatness, some with desktop computers on top, baskets of folders and papers, paper clips and pens, coffee cups and soda cans. None were exactly the same which made me think about elementary school and the way our teachers would expect us to keep our desks organized exactly the same way even though each one of us was markedly different, making our needs and uses for our desks consequently different.

The office was rather quiet, although I assumed that there had to be other rooms somewhere off of this one that held other people who didn't willingly show up here at the station, as my father and I had. I looked around timidly, hoping that we weren't disturbing anyone who was trying to concentrate on piecing together some evasive clues to solve some cold case or another. I don't know why I all of a sudden felt like our reason for being here wasn't worthy of the force's attention, but I knew that I was doing more than trying to solve my best friend's murder; I was protecting my own—my friends' well-being, my own word, my English teacher's reputation. The colors here were strong as different people walked in and out of the room from different doors, and I noticed that many of the colors centered on the body area instead of around the head. Blues and oranges shining from their throats down below their belly buttons. I wondered if this was the difference between people trying to get their versions of the truth out and the officers trying to decipher what in fact was truth and what they believed. I was studying my surroundings so intensely that I was lost in my own visions and was startled when Dad turned my face to his with both of his hands so that I was looking directly into his eyes, our noses almost touching.

"Violet. Violet, are you ready?" Dad asked, concern furrowed his brow.

I could see my distorted reflection in his eyes, gleaming with either tears or the overhead lights that were making me squint. "Yes. I'm ready."

We spoke with an investigator and two police officers, both of whom had been at school on Wednesday night for Winter Solstice. The one officer was the same one who had been talking to Cropsie in the cafeteria while Breck was being checked out. He was Officer Baker, and the other was Officer Becker. Their names were memorable to me not just because they sounded so similar, but because names can come from ways that families used to make a living. These two men probably didn't know it, but both of their families were probably bakers sometime somewhere long ago. I find that so interesting. What was I doing? Why was I thinking of mundane facts such as these officers' names? I was so exhausted that I was losing my mind. I was becoming certain of it.

Detective Monroe took notes while I spoke. I don't know why my mind kept wandering while I was talking. It was so important to me that the police had all of the background details surrounding Mindy's murder, alleged murder, they kept correcting. I was wondering whether the detective was French in origin, like the way Clay would make it out to be; I made a mental note that I should look up his last name sometime. I could hear my voice talking it all out, as if I were listening to someone else speaking. The voice was confident and sure. The facts came out in precise detail, and I watched the officers nod their heads at times agreeing with the scene we had all experienced.

I gave them my cell phone with its most recent list of text messages so that they could make records of the content and the source. The seven messages were not the same as the first set.

She lies
She cheats
She kills
She hates
She will pay
She will die
U no who

Even though I hadn't deleted the other text messages, the police had the resources to retrieve all the phone records from the service provider. They would be able to find out who sent them and when I received them. Unfortunately, even though I felt that they were threatening, the content of the messages themselves didn't really constitute threats. They included debatable offensive, accusatory language, but it was going to be my burden of proof that the sender was trying to annoy me or threaten me with these messages. And, now I was becoming confused about whether Alexis was talking about Ms. Stine or Mindy with this second set of messages.

"Did she ever admit to you that she sent any of these messages to scare you?" the detective asked, looking at his notes rather than at me.

"Not that I can remember," I said with a whine of frustration in my throat. "But she definitely was trying to start a fight with us at the mall, so that's threatening, right?" I asked, not really wanting an answer. "And that's when she sent the second set of texts."

The detective only nodded and kept his focus on his notes.

"Did she verbally or physically threaten you or your friends at the mall?" he asked, never affirming the rest of my answer to the prior question.

I had to think for a minute.

"Take your time," he added.

I was frustrated because now I was thinking that it was probably more Brittany who had been shouting at Mindy than Alexis doing the name-calling. The thing was I was sure that Alexis had put her up to it. Brittany had only been able to confront us because she had Alexis by her side. She never would've done anything like that alone.

"I guess it was both Alexis and Brittany. I don't know who exactly said what because I was so…so taken by surprise by their… uh…attack, I guess you could call it." I shrugged my shoulders feeling defeated and weak. I was so sure that Alexis was the true culprit, the criminal, the murderer even, and I was determined to gather the evidence to prove it true.

The confident voice that I had heard coming out of my mouth for the last hour was catching on these worries. I was frustrated as Detective Monroe asked me questions, and I felt like my answers weren't the ones that would bring Alexis in to face her crimes. They brought me a bottle of water, and I leaned back in the chair not realizing that my shoulders and back had turned stiff from sitting up so rigidly on the hard plastic. I took a few sips to coat the dryness in my mouth that kept returning with the growing panic that what I was sure was a clear case against Alexis may not turn out to be so.

Dad crossed and recrossed his arms over his chest as he listened to story after story. Some of the details among us hadn't surfaced to Dad until now. The night was getting late, and I wasn't offering much in terms of anything new once I had told them about all of my run-in's with Alexis and what I remembered from Winter Solstice. I was hoping at least that any answers to their questions regarding my relationship with Ms. Stine or my knowledge about her could only serve as being a fine character witness.

"I introduced my...my friend Breck to Ms. Stine during one of the concerts. We didn't talk for long, but she was the same as she always is. Nice, polite, nothing...nothing was wrong with her." I threw up my hands as if I was begging them to understand that she couldn't, would never do anything to hurt any of us. Not even Alexis. "She would never do anything to hurt any of her students. Not anyone at all, for that matter." The question jumped out, "Have you arrested her?"

"We can't answer your question, sorry." The detective looked up from his notes just then, and I was pretty sure that he hadn't arrested her from the soft look in his eyes and the tilt of his head. He quickly added, "We're just doing preliminary questioning right now, and your report here," he lifted his pad as if it were a trophy, "will help us find the facts and the guilty person or persons. So, it's been another long night, and I'm pretty satisfied with what we got from you here." He rose from his chair. Dad followed, so I stood up as well. He shook our hands with a firm handshake that crushed my knuckles together for a split second, although I didn't think he meant to do it. "If you have anything to add, just call." He handed Dad a business card. Dad thanked him, and I grabbed my half-empty bottle of water and followed them out of the office back into the first room.

Except for phones ringing and low conversations that I couldn't make out, the police station was the same as it had been as when we had arrived a couple hours earlier. I hoped I never had to come here again. My hands balled up in frustration because it felt like I was unable to help as I had wanted to. It had gotten much colder outside as Dad and I walked out into the night air. I shoved my fists under my armpits to keep them warm. Our breaths puffed in smoky clouds and pulled the cold air straight down into my lungs, which made me cough. The snow had stopped but had made the sidewalk slick with invisible ice. We linked arms and carefully made our way to the car.

It was almost 11:30, I noticed, when Dad started the car and turned the heat up as high as the fan would go.

"Sorry, Dad."

He looked at me confused before he put the car in gear. "For what, Violet?"

I sighed and felt the cough rise in my throat knowing that with it would become a sob and then tears again. "For everything. For worrying you. For keeping you up late before work again. For getting mixed up in this." I dropped my face into my hands and cried.

My father pulled the seatbelt across my shoulders and latched it in place which forced me to lift up my head. Although I still felt the cries in my throat, Dad lifted the violet from my neck and kissed it himself. I hadn't ever realized he thought about my violet enough to want to kiss it, even though it certainly would remind him of my mother just as much as it did me.

"You are all I have left, Vi. Don't ever apologize for the time I have to spend taking care of you. I know I work a lot and don't have a lot of time to spend with you. But I hope you know that I would spend every minute of the rest of my days with you if I had to." He kissed me on the forehead and then leaned back in his seat. He squeezed his hands around the steering wheel and looked out into the darkness of the parking lot. Like an umbrella, the street lamps' light encircled us, and our togetherness beamed.

"You hungry?" Dad asked. "Let's go get a big breakfast and sleep late tomorrow. I'm going to take the day off," his decision evident in his voice. "It's Friday before Christmas, and I think we deserve a nice long weekend together. What do you think?" he smiled at me and blinked his eyes slowly as if there were more to say behind those words, which there definitely was. We would have Mindy's funeral on Saturday.

"Blueberry waffles and hot chocolate," I said. And with that we drove away from the police station, leaving behind my worries and my words for the night at least.

I wasn't going to be able to prosecute Alexis on my own, of course, but Dad made me realize that I did all I was capable of to clear my teacher's name and to give the police the information that I had. It wasn't going to bring back my best friend either, and that was going to take a long time to handle. Maybe a lifetime. But I was sure of one thing, it was not going to take away another life, not mine, not Breck's or Clay's, not Ms. Stine's. And, I was not going to spend my life worrying about the possibility. I was going to shine some light on the darkness myself.

This paper reminded me of the earth, lush and brown with a mossy softness to the touch, as if a plant or a squirrel would settle right into it.

My Little Violet,
Don't wish your life away. Before you know it, you'll be older than you want to be.

Chapter 16

THE funeral was over.

The beautiful day was unrelenting and such sharp contrast to the darkness that was shrouding my insides. The sun glowed splendidly, luxurious orange and a warm pink despite the chill of December. We stood in the cemetery, the minister's words ended and left us wanting reassurance that we could accept this tragedy and go on with our everyday details.

I left my sunglasses over my dry eyes, too distraught to cry, too dismayed that no one was blaming the guilty. Dad stood behind me at the gravesite and leaned over to whisper in my ear that he'd be ready to leave whenever I was and that I could take as long or as little as I liked here with my friends. Without my best friend.

I was holding onto Breck's hand with both of mine, and I leaned my head against his shoulder not able to say anything back to Dad. I turned to him and nodded that I had heard him, and then I looked back at the site where Mindy was being lowered into the ground. Although with the deluge of people, I was finding it hard to hone in on my own feelings and block out all the colors and thoughts that inundate me at times like this. I tried to calm myself by breathing in my violet, as I held it to my lips for almost the entire service. I was unable to focus entirely on the funeral, which in this case wasn't all bad, considering how I felt. Mindy's family was in all states of grief: silent and stricken, sobbing and hysterical, confused and vengeful. And, Clay, Breck and I were feeling this combination as well.

We left the family with a few words, mostly from Clay, who expressed his condolences once again for us. A lot of teachers and school counselors were present, and they all made mention that we could call them for help, if we needed to talk to someone about how we were feeling. I tugged at Breck's hand and led him away from the gravesite to the path that led back to the parking area. I couldn't look at Mindy's family any longer without my violet necklace strangling my breath, or it may have been the lump of loss in my own throat. The black of my dress billowed behind me as I swung around to face the crowd gathered here for Mindy. I spotted Ms. Stine quiet and hidden in the throngs of people, but I wanted to make sure she didn't leave without our sharing with her the fact that we knew she was innocent.

I continued to drag Breck with me as I called her name. "Ms. Stine. Ms. Stine." Not being very tall, I'm sure she was unsure about who was calling her and whether she wanted to wait around to see who it was. "Ms. Stine," I said again, and she spotted me.

"Violet, I'm so sorry," she said softly, bowing her head.

"I'm sorry, too. I...I...just want you to know, well, I didn't want you to think that I...that we...," I was panting as if I were running and couldn't catch my breath.

"I know, Violet," she said, as she lifted her sunglasses onto her head and looked me in the eyes. Her sorrow was easily visible on her face and in the blue shadows that burst out around her. But I saw hope there too. "If we don't learn from history, we're bound to repeat it, right?"

I nodded, but I needed to tell her what I knew. "Right, but this is different. You're not to blame here." I spread my arms out and looked around at everyone trying to comfort each other.

"You'll see, Violet. It'll all work out." She replaced her sunglasses over her eyes, and I realized I hadn't noticed their color. But the sad blue shadows that veiled her hair and her back, twinkled with violet just then. I cocked my head to the side and watched her walk through the people, disappearing in the sea of black mourning clothes. I must've stayed like that for some time stuck in a vision that I was trying to reconstruct from Ms. Stine's colors. There was something familiar there, comforting yet elusive. I guess I was just amazed that she could be so optimistic when she could be accused of murder if Alexis' guilt could not be confirmed.

Austin broke my gaze. "What does she have to say?" he asked, pointing to Ms. Stine with his thumb and looking over his shoulder at her with accusation in his tone.

For the first time, I was skeptical of Austin's underlying purpose. He was at the mall. He knows that Brittany and Alexis are friends and that Mindy was expecting to meet up with him at Winter Solstice. I was surprised that he wouldn't have already acknowledged Ms. Stine's unfortunate position she has been dealt in this tragedy that Alexis orchestrated.

"What do you mean, Austin?" I said, confronting him. "Ms. Stine is hoping that the guilty party will be found out. You know who she means, don't you?"

"Well, Alexis isn't the only one to blame. I was talking to Brittany, and she said that Ms. Stine was giving her a hard time over transferring classes." I was appalled that he would pick this time to readmit Brittany to his life.

"Really, Austin? Teachers can disagree with scheduling issues. That's not what we're talking about here. We're talking about a mean, sick girl who killed my friend, our friend," I emphasized.

He shrugged his shoulders. He was making me so mad. "You don't know that for sure," he said and walked away. The gold that I had always associated with him was tarnished green, like when copper turns when exposed to the elements. Maybe he was trying to make sense of it for himself and Brittany sought out his attention. That had to be it. Otherwise, Austin wasn't who I thought he was.

Now I really had to get out of here. Breck was just going to go home with Dad and me, because his dad was closing on our neighbor's house. We planned to stop at Mindy's house again for a short visit, and then we would try to relax at home. Clay joined us to hitch a ride over to Mindy's because his parents were not going to go over from the funeral.

There were a lot more people at Mindy's today than there had been the other night. People were bringing all kinds of food, dishes of foiled covered casseroles, plates of sliced cakes, and bowls of fruits and salads of all sizes. Dad left us in the kitchen to find the men watching football and having drinks in the den. After finding it hard to maneuver around all the people, Breck and I stepped outside on the patio through the sliding glass doors from the kitchen. I felt that I could breathe out here, even though the contradiction of the bright sunshine warming us on such a cold day emotionally was enough to take my breath away. Breck just held me from behind and kissed me on my cheek when I looked up at his face. His arms kept me warm on the outside. Inside I was frozen, not knowing how we were all going to go back to school without Mindy and with all of this misinformation and discord rumbling just under the surface.

"You must be sorry you met me," I said. I couldn't turn around to face Breck then, even though I wanted to see what I could see in his eyes and listen closely to his thoughts. His colors were still a violet that merged smoothly with mine.

"Well, since you mentioned it...," he said. I whipped around then to catch his smile, as he was trying to hold in a laugh. He hugged me to his chest and whispered in my ear, "You have no idea how glad I am that you are so curious about houses for sale." This time I laughed.

Clay came outside then. "Am I interrupting?"

I laughed a little nervously. Then Breck said, with his sense of humor that I was becoming able to predict, "Of course you're interrupting! Get out of here, will ya'? Jeez..." Clay laughed with Breck and pretended he was trying to step in between us. I gave Clay a good, strong hug, because I was sure he needed it, although he'd never admit to it behind his comic façade.

Clay invited us back inside as the suggestion was made to go over to the football game scheduled for this afternoon. "Do you want to go? I mean, would going be disrespectful to Mindy? Or, Violet, are you worried about running into Alexis and her entourage there?"

Although we expected we might have to see her, we agreed that Mindy would not want Alexis to rule our lives. "It might be good for us to go, to feel a little better, even though I still miss Mindy so much." I started crying unexpectedly then, thinking about all the things Mindy and I have done together that we'll never do again, ever. Breck cradled my head against him, and assured me that it was going to be a long time before the urge to cry would go away. And that was just going to be the way it was. I wiped the tears away on my sleeve, knowing he was right.

We went back in to find my dad and tell him that we wanted to go over to the football game at school. He wasn't completely thrilled with the idea, but he knew there would probably be extra security there after the incident at Winter Solstice. So, Dad said he'd take us as long as we agreed to go back to my house after the game. He'd pick up some pizzas for us, and we could watch football on TV and just hang out and spend Christmas Eve together.

"Your dad is pretty cool, Violet," Breck said.

"Yeah, thanks. I think so," I said, kind of feeling proud of him for stepping out of his own comfort zone and being willing to participate in our events with us. I wanted Dad to know that was what I thought too, but I felt a little awkward saying so in front of Breck. It made me feel embarrassed like when my friends first saw my parents, and I just wanted to deny that I belonged to them for some stupid adolescent reason, like their clothes are the wrong brand or their hair is the wrong style. Instead, I gave Dad a kiss on the cheek as we said good-bye's once again to some of Mindy's family and piled into Dad's car. Dad looked at me a little strangely, but I saw the hint of a smile that satisfied me. *I love you too, Violet.*

It was cold sitting at the football game, but it felt good to be outside, letting the breeze and the sun tickle our faces and cheering in our loudest voices when the ball was going in our favor. The yelling released some of my mixed up emotions; it let me laugh and cry in frustration but blame it on the game. We stayed well into the fourth quarter when it was clear that our team was not going to win today. I felt bad for the players, because it must be hard to concentrate for any of them who were directly affected by the most recent events. There were still quite a few students walking around with bandages or some other sort of evidence that they had been injured Wednesday night. Clay spent a large part of the second half of the game walking around talking to people, as he was good at doing, and he reported that most everyone appeared to have calmed down since Winter Solstice and were trying to put it behind them.

I didn't feel bad for Austin though, as I watched him throw inaccurate passes and get pushed to the ground a few times. I didn't want him to get hurt; he was my friend, I still believed. But, he didn't seem to be on my side. I wondered what that meant for our court case that we'd resume in January. I didn't want to think about that now, as it made me dread the fact that Alexis may still show her face in our English class.

Clay asked us to drop him off on our way home from the game, in the spirit that we had had enough for one day. That was an understatement. I understood, but I was grateful for his sticking around and befriending Breck. We wished him a merry Christmas, which was tomorrow after all. His family had plans for Christmas Eve anyway, and we agreed that we would meet up some day before New Year's. That reminded me that Mindy was interested in Austin's company for New Year's Eve, which added heat to my smoldering anger towards him all the more. Mindy wasn't begging for his attention but was definitely interested in it, and here he was denying that her murderer was guilty.

Dad stopped by Pierro's on our way home and ordered a couple pizzas to fulfill our range of tastes. Breck liked any kind of peppers, hot and sweet, and onions. The spicier, the better, he claimed, giving me a silly look that I couldn't help but to smile at. I could handle the spicy pizza. I was also growing rather fond of Breck. I remember meeting him and liking his confidence and casualness when he talked to me that first day in Mrs. Suden's house when he was baking those chocolate chip cookies to fill the house with the homemade smell. I worry though when I think that a tragedy may have drawn us together. I've heard of that before— when two people overcome some hardship or live through some life-threatening event, it brings them together. Just as it can break them apart. Instead of actually having interests in common or liking each other for their personality traits, it's possible that we don't really have any connection other than the loss of Mindy and living through the terror of being at school when she died. I hope that it's more than that. I like his humor and the way he seems to care about me. I think Dad has picked up on that as well. Dad seems to be treating Breck as if we've known him for longer than we have. I guess Dad trusts my judgment to a certain extent, but since Dad has also met his parents and he knows that they treated me well the night everything transpired at school, he has reason to accept Breck.

Dad agreed to ordering pizza with peppers and onions, although he liked plain cheese. When we all went inside to wait for the order, he asked Breck what kind his father liked.

"I expect him to stop over after the closing on the house next door, so what's his preference?" Dad asked Breck.

"He's pretty easy when it comes to food. Whatever you order will be fine, sir, I'm sure," answered Breck.

I thought Breck was being polite by not making requests, and I noticed his respectful manners right away. I'm sure Dad did. So, we brought home a variety along with a couple sodas and a six-pack of beer and sat around our living room eating at the coffee table in front of the TV watching a college football bowl game. I was outvoted in my request to watch *Miracle on 34th Street*, which is one of my favorite Christmas specials. I poured us some sodas, Dad a beer, and Breck's parents arrived just as we were getting started.

I greeted them at the door. Breck's mom handed me a pie.

"I hope you like pumpkin," she said. She headed right by me to my father and handed him a bottle of red wine. "And, I hope you like red."

"Thank you, Kris. Jack." He switched the wine bottle to his left hand and greeted Breck's father with another strong hand-shake. I guess it was easy to see where Breck's manners came from. His parents came inside and easily made themselves comfortable.

Dad poured some wine and gave Breck's father a beer. They served themselves pizza and followed us into the living room where Breck hadn't moved away from the television. Breck did stand up from his spot on the floor leaning against the coffee table to kiss his mother hello. She gave him one of her two slices of pizza from her plate and sat in one of our softest chairs that has a small ottoman in front of it. She laid her plate on it and sipped her wine without touching her pizza while the men chatted about today's football game and compared it to the game we were watching. I made conversation with Breck's mother about Christmas and what they usually do on Christmas Eve. They didn't have any traditions, she said, except for going to visit family who was scattered around the country. Since Breck's dad had several house sales going, they stayed in town this holiday, which suited her just fine she said as she got up from her chair to pour herself another glass of wine. I noticed her pizza still lay on the ottoman.

Talk of Breck's dad selling the house interested me some. He told Dad and me that we'd be happy with our new neighbors he guessed. They were a young family with one little baby, very different from Mrs. Suden and her empty house. I wondered if the new baby would have the space that was my bedroom or not. Like the way we turned our nursery into a multi-purpose room with the treadmill and Mom's old hobbies packed away. Or, maybe they would have a second child. I hoped for this child, whom I didn't even know, the gift of having a sibling, someone other than its parents to talk to, play with, dream with. I looked forward to meeting them. I wondered what Mom would have taken over to them to welcome them to the neighborhood. I'd have to think about it some more. I don't remember her ever doing that before, but I know it would be something she'd do. One of those nice things that comes back to you someday. Maybe a basket of stuff.

As the football game got boring, the parlor called to me. I wiped my hands on a napkin and took a sip of soda. Without trying to draw any attention to myself, I sneaked across the room to the piano. I'm not sure why I didn't feel embarrassed this time sitting down to play piano in front of Breck, not to mention his parents, but I felt ready to play for him. It was like I needed him to hear my music. It would help me feel closer to Mom.

I played softly, just some warming up, like Mom and I would do first. Breck's mom walked in and sat where Dad often sits to listen in the chair by the window.

"Do you mind?" she asked.

"Of course not," I answered, and I meant it. For the first time in a while, I really just wanted to play. The melody flowed from my fingertips, that familiar melody that just comes to my mind and out of my body. The silver dust sprinkled the air, although I closed my eyes to it. The music took my mind away from missing Mom and from missing Mindy. Instead I felt the music was unblocking other colors, other visions, opening a path to communicate with Mom, but she was just out of my reach. I kept playing, my violet brightening against my chest, turning from shades of violet to pink like a sinking sunset.

I looked at the book of songs open in front of me, and the pink shone like a spotlight onto the pages, and I knew where the answer lay. The pink blended darker to purple and even deeper to indigo, highlighting the harmony between the music I was playing and the realizations overtaking me. Dust shimmered in the rays of light and entranced me to the point where I forgot that I had an audience. I saw the notes flowing up and down fluidly, guiding my fingers just the same on the piano keys. The pressure I put on the keys reflected the energy. I was ridding myself of the despair as if I were under a spell. I felt hopeful, just as I sensed Breck join his mother in listening to me. As if he had his own violet, I knew he was smiling. Without turning around, I ended the song with a bow of my head and a settling on the last chord that drifted into the evening without urgency. Time felt normal now. We could just enjoy Christmas Eve without its being charged with unwelcome feelings.

She must have used this stationery to write notes to her piano students. It had music staffs on it in rainbow colors.

My Little Violet,
Music is a universal language. Let it speak to you when no one else can.

Chapter 17

IT was one of those nights that felt like snow. As Dad said good night to Breck's parents, I walked down the sidewalk to the curb with Breck. Without a coat, it was certainly cold, and I shivered.

Breck said, "You don't have to do that just to get a hug and kiss from me."

Just as I was trying to argue with him that I hadn't shivered deliberately, he kissed me, right in front of our parents. "You have to admit it was a good idea," I said, even though he knew I hadn't done it on purpose.

He laughed, "Which idea—the shiver or the kiss?"

I just shook my head. Except for the fact that my mom wasn't here to share it with us, it was a pretty good Christmas Eve. "Merry Christmas, Breck."

"Merry Christmas, Violet." He kissed me on my nose and then looked up. Tiny snowflakes were just beginning to fall from the night sky, gracefully ending our evening together. "Can I see you tomorrow?"

"That would be a great Christmas present," I said.

The Stewarts hugged me and hurried into the car to warm up. I ran back into the house, and Dad shut the door behind me. We both shook off the snowflakes.

"I don't believe I expected to have such a nice Christmas Eve," Dad said.

"Me either." I lifted myself onto my tiptoes and gave Dad a big squeeze around the neck. "I love you, Dad."

"I love you too, Vi." He sighed. I know he was thinking about Mom just then, but the night was spread with more cheer than last year this time. "Let's clean up and get to bed. Don't want to be awake when Santa comes, now do we?" Now that Dad was joking around, I knew that it had been a good night for him too. That pleased me.

While we put away the leftover pizza and pumpkin pie, Dad commented on my piano playing. He was surprised that I was willing to play in front of people who were basically strangers.

"It's easier, I guess, to play in front of people who you don't think will judge you," I said. "Plus, as bad as things have been," I swallowed thoughts of Mindy, "the music was struggling to come out. It helped me see…, Dad, you know, see the colors clearly. It helped me listen to the thoughts."

Heading upstairs, I decided to take a hot shower to relax and try to clear my head for sleep. Sleep for me had not been restful, what little of it I had been able to get. I felt like I hadn't spent a full night in my bed for a week. Almost anyway.

As the steam filled the bathroom from the hot spray of the shower, I looked at myself in the mirror. I wanted to tell Mom that I didn't feel like her little girl anymore, the one who was afraid of dogs in the yard and wanted her to braid my hair and let me wear my dresses even when we were just going to the grocery store. I had more loss than some adults have had, I suspected. I closed my eyes and unhooked my violet from my neck. I was going to let my mind rest and take a few moments in the shower for myself. I laid it carefully next to the sink on a tissue so that it wouldn't slide anywhere. I resisted the thoughts that plagued me: Alexis, Austin, Mindy, Mom. And, I stepped into the hot water pelting my face and neck, turning around so that it could pound my back and shoulders. I just stood there and waited for the water to take away the pain. I knew that taking off my violet necklace wouldn't seal off the colors and made them invisible to me. But I just wanted to check to be sure. I knew the gift was in me. I started to sing in the shower.

Then, as if a waterfall itself showered into my vision, I saw her. Mom knew that Mindy had passed and wanted to tell me something. Her rose-colored shape was unmistakable; I knew it was she. I rubbed the water out of my eyes and tried to blink. Wider and wider I opened my eyes. There was still blackness and the rose candle lit in the middle, flickering soundlessly but waving as if it were talking to me. I left the water on, stepped out onto the lavender bath rug and grabbed my towel off its rack to wipe my eyes dry. I leaned over to reach my violet necklace hoping that I could get more information from Mom and my vision if I had it around my neck. Still singing softly, I stepped onto the tile floor with one foot to be able to reach it. Despite my forethought to place it on a tissue so that it wouldn't slide down the drain, my foot slipped on the tile, and instead of having a hold of my violet, I swept it right down the drain in one swift motion.

There was barely anything else that could tick me off about now. I turned off the shower and sat down on the bathroom rug and cried. For my mother. For Dad having to live without her too. For Austin for not having the strength to stand up for himself. For finding Breck and being happy but knowing that Mindy would never be happy like that. The vision of Mom vanished then, in my sobs, the tears flushing away whatever it was she was trying to tell me. I'd have to get my violet before getting in bed. So much for a long night's sleep. I knew I wouldn't be able to sleep without it though.

I wrapped the towel around my wet hair and put on my bathrobe to go and find Dad. Leaving the door open to the bathroom warmed the cool hallway with steam and spread light so that I could see that Dad had already fallen asleep in his bed with the

TV on. I couldn't bear to wake him knowing that he had been worrying about me and probably not getting much sleep. Not that the recent events would have taken more of a toll on him than the last year had.

I had no clue how to unscrew the pipe underneath the sink to get my necklace out. I knew that I wouldn't lose my necklace altogether, but it was a hopeless task to try to do it myself. It would have to wait until morning.

I walked to my bedroom and combed my wet hair, put on some flannel pants and a cotton tee to sleep in. Hanging my towel back up in the bathroom, I opened the cabinet under the sink just in case my necklace was magically sitting there for me to get back. It wasn't. I brushed my teeth and went to bed. It would be the first night that I can ever remember sleeping without my violet around my neck.

I had to go downstairs to the parlor and try to play from Mom's music book to see if I could reach her. Quietly, so that I would awaken Dad, I played. One song. Then another. Then one more. I turned through the music, especially choosing pages that matched Mindy's melon, but it was no use. I was trying too hard, so I just went up to bed exhausted.

I didn't think I'd have any dreams that night, but I was wrong. What I remember most about the dream was the sound of the wind. It reminded me of the dream I had when I lost Mindy. It was so loud rushing in my ears that I couldn't hear anything else. No talking. No screaming. No breathing. Just the wind as fierce as any storm I could remember that would unleash torrents of rain from low thick clouds that made it cold and dark so all I wanted to do was stay indoors. But I was outside, and the clouds were rolling in on the wind as if they were sailing in on waves. Then, suddenly the air was filled with pages from books. Pink, red, black, melon, green, purple. I found myself trying to notice the colors instead of being scared of being caught out in the storm without shelter or even a coat or an umbrella. I started running against the wind, through the flutter of pages surrounding me, batting them out of my way as I shielded my eyes with my hand over my forehead like a visor. I knew where I was headed and I felt as if I was almost there. The rose-colored angel twinkling in lights. There she was. I could see her down the road. I kept running. The clouds were overtaking me from behind, making the air thick so it was harder to lift my legs, making the air dark so it was harder to see. The rain had stopped and I was looking all around for colors. The pages were still floating by me, but now they were all white, like the colors were being covered up. I knew the colors were still there for me to see, to read, but the white was denying me the scene. My legs were tiring, the colors had faded, and I couldn't reach the angel there before me by myself. I slowed down and searched for something. Someone. I needed help, and I knew it was there. But I was falling asleep, my mind becoming drowsy in such harsh wind. Too much oxygen. I couldn't catch my breath. I was falling to the ground, fainting, sleeping. And the white pages were floating in the waning wind, slowing to rest on top of my body, like a blanket covering me while I slept.

I awoke to the aroma of coffee, so I knew Dad was up already. And, it still seemed early because the light wasn't streaming through my bedroom window. I rolled over to look at the picture of Mom. I gave her a morning kiss by kissing the tips of my fingers and touching her face in the picture frame. Looking beyond the photograph, I noticed that I hadn't closed my closet all the way, and I saw just the corner of the silver box I had taken from the flower shop sitting on the floor inside its folding doors where I had left it when we finally had made it home from the hospital. Thinking about the vivid dream I had, now I wondered whether the gift my parents said I had was truly mine and not some extension of the violet that embraced the black cord with its shimmering leaves. As much as I wanted to lie in bed longer and maybe fall back asleep again, I wanted to retrieve my violet from the sludge that it probably slept in inside the sink pipe. And, I wanted to tell Dad about my dream and what I needed to do.

Even though I had a good night's sleep, I descended the stairs slowly in a daze, my mind preoccupied with my dream and releasing my violet from its trap. Looking out the window of the parlor as I arrived down on the first floor, I noticed it had snowed. Just enough to coat the grass in the yards but melt on the street and the sidewalks. Little white spots like Christmas cookies were baked onto the window frozen instead of warm. I walked up to the window, hearing Dad turning the pages of the newspaper in the kitchen, and looked outside knowing that the present I wanted would be delivered, although I would have to make it happen; no one else was going to be able to bring it to me. It looked heavenly outside, frigid icing waiting to be melted into sugar crystals by the sun. I wrapped my arms around my body feeling the chill just on the other side of the window, and looking forward to the day, I greeted Dad in the kitchen.

"Merry Christmas, Dad."

"Merry Christmas, Vi. How'd you sleep?" he asked, as if he knew the details of my dream were dripping off my tongue. So, I described it to him over a cup of hot chocolate.

He nodded his head as if caught up by my description, imagining the scene in his own mind, but not sure what to make of it.

"I have to tell the detectives about her notebook, the Slam Book," I told Dad.

"I understand, sweetheart, but they probably wouldn't be available being Christmas Day, you know." He knew he was disappointing me with his logic, but I knew he was right. Between playing the piano earlier and seeing the color illuminate my song book reminded me about that disgusting book of hers that furnished more evil, and I was positive that my dream sealed her guilt. Alexis and her motive were crystal clear to me, no fog in the way.

I let it go for now and moved on to the next issue that betrayed my sleeping late. Dad led the way upstairs to my bathroom. He lay on the tile floor halfway inside the cabinet, pushing the toilet paper rolls and the extra box of tissues out of the way. He yelped as he was trying to adjust himself around the pipe with enough circumference to wield the trap off the other sections of the pipe. Without bumping his head, just scraping his back he said, he sat up and dumped my wet necklace out of the trap onto the hand towel he had instructed I hold. I was relieved to have it back in my possession and vowed to be more careful, which probably meant that I wouldn't ever take it off again. He replaced the curved section of the pipe so that I could rinse off my necklace. I dried it carefully in the hand towel, noticing that the white veins were appearing almost silver in the tender petals of the flower, which made me think of clever ways to go about taking care of everything. I sighed with an audible breath as I hung my necklace back around my neck where it belonged.

Dad and I didn't have too much in the house to make an event of breakfast this morning, but I was able to fry a few eggs and toast slices of multigrain bread that hadn't been in the freezer too long. I poured an inch of coffee into my cold hot chocolate to warm it up and took my fresh mocha into the parlor to play a few Christmas carols while Dad put the dishes in the dishwasher and straightened up the kitchen.

When Dad joined me in the parlor and sat in his chair by the window to listen to my playing, I was charged. I played firmly and with conviction and even sang along to a verse of "Winter Wonderland." I looked behind me and saw Dad sip his coffee and lean his head back in the high-backed chair with some sense of satisfaction on his face. I hadn't seen that kind of peace in him in over a year.

I'm not sure how long I played, but I eventually stopped to get dressed and brush my teeth, knowing that Mom had led me in the right direction even if it was through my dream. She still had more to tell me though; I didn't have all the pieces put together yet. Along with finding a way to tell the detectives about Alexis' Slam Book, I wanted to finish reading *To Kill A Mockingbird* today if I could. I wondered how Ms. Stine was spending her break from school. She never says much about her personal life, so it would be hard to say if there is anyone to comfort her for the loss of one of her students and the accusation she might face if the police gather enough evidence against her instead of suspecting another guilty party in Mindy's death.

I curled up in the sunshine I found in the parlor through the window, and I finished the novel early in the afternoon. I knew I'd have to return to it to help make sense of all of the resolutions, but I felt accomplished for the day. And, I was going to be ready to put Alexis to the test in our class' court trial if she was going to be participating. There was no way a liar like her would escape being condemned. I felt like I had proof, but I would have to ponder that more.

Breck called around lunchtime to see what my plans were for the day. I didn't tell him about my dream, but I did tell him I had a restless night from dropping my necklace down the drain. He promised that he'd get me a new one should I ever lose it. I didn't have the heart to tell him that even if he did, it couldn't ever be replaced. It was my tie to Mom. And that wasn't replaceable. I think I needed Mom's help in some way, according to my dream, and my music wasn't doing the job. I was afraid that Alexis would never come to trial. And, I couldn't let Mindy down like that.

Mom's paper was as true blue as the sky where it meets a Caribbean sea that's clear to the bottom, and I cannot tell the difference.

My Little Violet,
Sometimes the best tool is a good plan.

Chapter 18

AFTER spending the morning with his parents, Breck came over to our house. We decided to go for a walk in the frigid, fresh air of the afternoon. This winter day was one of those that I always wonder how it can look so hot outside from the inside, but once I've stepped outside, my skin burns from the cold. The sun looked so strong, but it barely heated my body. I shoved my gloved hands into the pockets of my winter jacket to shield them further as we walked through the vanishing puffs our breaths made. I wore my knit hat and matching scarf in a shade of plum that complimented the charcoal gray of my jacket. Breck pulled me closer by the waist as we strolled down the sidewalk slippery wet with a glaze of melting snow. The sun was soothing. I noticed how it relieved the trees of the snow piled precariously on their spindly twigs, left bare to the winter's weather. I felt like that tree today— balancing the snow dumped on top of me and hoping the sun would assume the burden and remove it before I noticed its weight too much. We didn't talk too much about what was really on my mind, missing Mindy and making sure Alexis' guilt was found out. The walk was good though; it was like a vitamin that invigorated me, and I soon wasn't feeling the cold from the exercise.

I had to pull my hat off my head and stuffed it into my pocket because I was beginning to get so warm. I separated my scarf from my face to let my warm breath out and a bit of the cool air in.

Breck unzipped his coat too. Having decided to turn around to head back to my house for hot chocolate and a snack, we saw Cropsie coming towards us carrying a felt tote bag in his hand. It couldn't have been very heavy by the way he was swinging it by his side. I wasn't quite sure where he could've been shopping on Christmas Day as stores and most restaurants were closed for the holiday.

Without any mention to me that he was going to, Breck called out to him. I touched Breck's arm in curiosity, but not in time to ask him what I was wondering. I listened instead.

"Merry Christmas, sir," he said with a polite wave.

"Merry Christmas to you," Cropsie replied with a clear voice.

It still stunned me to hear Cropsie speak. I always imagined a gruff, gravelly grunt from him as if he could barely understand how to answer another person with respect. It made me embarrassed in my ignorance and misjudgment. I looked away pretending to notice the icicles dripping off the tree branches overhead.

"Merry Christmas," I stuttered, as I tried to hide my gaze from his.

As he passed us, he spoke again, and I saw the gold. "I'm sorry."

Then, I had to meet his eyes. In surprise, I answered, "Yes, sir. Thank you." I figured he meant for the loss of Mindy.

"Your mother was lovely," he said. He reached in his bag and handed Breck and me each a candy cane and continued on his way.

I looked after him. I bet my mouth was literally hanging open because Breck was staring at me.

"What?" Breck asked in a whisper.

I shrugged my shoulders. I didn't know what to say. I was ashamed for never having given Cropsie a chance. I was just as guilty as Alexis, when I thought about it, while we walked back home to Dad.

I must've been walking as if in a trance, submerged in my own self-loathing. Before I realized it, Breck had bent over to grab a handful of snow that he packed into a firm ball in his palms and tossed it with good intentions right at me. I turned just in time to let it smash into powder on the back of my jacket. I laughed incredulously at him as I saw him already forming his next snowball. I intended to get him back, but I wasn't quick enough between the surprise attack and my slow reaction time when it came to things like throwing balls and other sports. He had already launched number two by the time I got my first one out of my hand.

As if I was ever very good at throwing any sort of ball, one that doesn't stay intact was more challenging, so my side of the battle was quickly showing defeat. I raised my hands in surrender.

"Ok, ok, I give up." I was breathing hard in the cold air from trying to defend myself.

Breck strutted up to me in victory, and I punched him playfully on the shoulder. "You ready to head back?" He pulled me close so that I couldn't punch him again.

I shook my head. Breck cocked his head to the side with that cocker spaniel puppy kind of confusion. The one that said I thought I was getting all the attention, so what do you mean you're not giving me all of yours. I hooked my arm in his and trudged through the slush on the sidewalk down the street the few blocks to Cropsie's house. I had no plan, no spell. Just a purpose and a message to deliver.

I took a deep breath and patted my violet subconsciously on my chest; although it was under the thickness of my jacket, I felt it brighten with the courage I was drawing from it. I stood with Breck at the bottom of the steps that rose up to Cropsie's porch. From far away, I thought it was aging, rickety, like it would creak with each breath of the wind, like the one in *To Kill A Mockingbird*. It still surprised me as I approached but with its cleanliness.

I was stuck in such a spell just studying his porch. Not a drop of snow on the cement floor, not a haze of dust or dirt on the windows, not a strip of paint missing from a shutter or the trim. It was meticulously kept. I glanced back at Breck, not because I needed him to support me or protect me, but because I wished I could put in words all of the amazement rushing through me standing here in Cropsie's forbidden territory. I never would have guessed I'd have the courage or the desire.

I knocked on the door with my right hand, my left hand still resting on my chest where my violet necklace lay beneath my jacket, protected, protecting me. Behind the glass of the storm door, I sensed he was approaching. I felt my breath stop for a second as the old wooden door opened. The door had three windows above my line of sight, glass diamonds. I couldn't see him, but I saw his colors. He was alone but in his proper place. His golden yellow was stoic and well thought out; I wasn't surprising him with my interests.

He was going to let me speak first. He had no words to waste.

I realized I didn't know how to address him. Mr. Cropsie? I didn't even really know if that was his name. So that was it, I finally understood.

I extended my hand in a formal handshake. Before now, he always seemed untouchable. But, I figured, I was the one who seemed that way to him. "I'm Violet. Rose's daughter. You must've known her." He just looked at me with nothing in his expression to read. Just his yellow thoughts reaching out to me.

"Christopher," he said. I guessed that was his introduction to me as he gave me a stiff nod. I still didn't know if that was his first name or last, but at least I knew something. Then, he stepped right by me and addressed Breck. "Your father's sold that house?" He gestured down the street where my house stood.

Breck stuttered trying to gather an answer quickly, not sure why we were talking to Cropsie in the first place. "Yes. Yes, sir."

Cropsie just waited, looking at Breck, as if there were another probing question blinking in the air on some billboard that he could see and we couldn't.

So Breck continued. "A small family. With a baby, I think." He shrugged his shoulders more in embarrassment than not knowing the facts.

Cropsie just nodded. We were all standing there, like snowmen, stiff and uncomfortable and unable to move on their own yet wanting to get out of the heat. It was awkward. So awkward that I didn't even want to shift my position and draw more attention to the fact that I was still standing on Cropsie's porch with him no more than six inches from my personal space. The words finally came to me in a fumbling heap. "If there is ever anything I can do for you to help you or if you need something...I just wanted you to know."

"I know." That was all he said. And it was with that, we had connected. Two people as different as two could be, yet I think he knew that I appreciated him for letting me thank him on his turf. I think he had had a softness for my mother or something like that, and now I had made a connection. A connection he fought to keep away but silently needed and didn't know how to ask for.

No more words were spoken then, but I knew that I would remember this conversation. It was the first time that I could recall that I was truly surprised by someone's intentions, because usually I could see them coming. Or read them in the colors.

We arrived back home to find Dad warm and surprised that I was content even though I was soaked and cold in places where the snow had seeped into my jacket and knit gloves. He squinted his eyes just a little at me while Breck and I were saying good-bye; it was his sign of approval of Breck and how he was treating me. Dad was glad I was finding energy in happiness, in a friendship, being without Mom and now without Mindy too.

Dad wandered off to give us a little privacy. Breck's dad was next door at the neighbor's, so Breck was going over to help him pack up some of the knick-knacks that they use to stage the house as if people are actually living there. Some of the pictures are actually of Breck and his relatives.

"Before I go, I wanted to give you something for Christmas," Breck said, with a little nervousness coloring his cheeks with pink. He didn't meet my eyes even at the moment that his fingers touched mine. He dropped the small white jewelry box into my hand. It was tied simply with a strand of purple gift ribbon that curled up when stretched with the blade of a scissors on the striated side. I couldn't guess what it was, but I knew Breck was hoping I'd like it.

I pulled at the ribbon and held it in my fist, removing the lid halfway, and looking at him with wide eyes, wondering if what was inside was going to change our relationship. Breck looked at me and then back at the box. I uncovered a pair earrings, sparkling cubes on posts that would nestle on my earlobes. Frozen inside each of the cubes, as if their lives could continue forever, was a tiny violet. They were so perfect. I couldn't believe that Breck found something that was as meaningful as it was, to reflect who I was. He made me feel proud to be so different. I never felt that way as a result of someone other than my parents, until now.

It made me anxious, but it gave me strength.

I impatiently waited till the next day to start taking care of business. Out of respect for the holiday, I waited. But as soon as I woke up, I needed to get started. Dad had to go back to work today, so that left me alone to get anything accomplished regarding solving Mindy's murder.

Clay and I were texting back and forth. He had been questioned by the police and told them about the Slam Book. I'm sure that if Clay could have dressed in some detective garb, like a Sherlock Holmes cape pretending to smoke a huge pipe, the curve of it bigger than his hand, he would have followed through just for the joke. He said that they had heard about the book from several students but hadn't located it.

I was sure with that evidence that Alexis would be accused with reasonable cause. I went upstairs to get the book, Mom's book. I had removed it from the piano after Christmas, sure that it was more powerful than a music book. I was still so afraid every time I opened its cover that the panic would rise in my stomach and make me hate my gift. I tried to ignore the unfairness of it. These feelings that made me spin out of control in a crowd overcome by all the colors swirling, twirling me tighter so that I couldn't breathe. I had never asked for this. Already I felt responsible for Mindy. The problem with Alexis's colors is they were so different, contradictory. They weren't hues of the same basic color. I lay the book on the kitchen table next to my half eaten breakfast—a small glass that held the grapefruit juice I had squeezed out of the half I had eaten and a blueberry yogurt I had barely touched.

I went directly to the darkest colors in the book. The ones in the back that really scared me. Shiny black pages, waxy and smooth. Charcoal pages that were dull and grainy. Ash and stone, pages flecked with such small dots of black and gray that I had to run my palms over them to feel the tiny bumps. There were none. Only the music notes were raised from the pages. The notes must hold the power in the secret harmonies they sang.

Without singing any of them aloud for fear I would unleash something dangerous and hurt someone else I loved, I went over the tune in my head. It wasn't what I was looking for. I couldn't explain it; it didn't help me see or hear anything.

My phone was interrupting me with texts from Clay. I asked him if he had ever gotten to ask Austin why he didn't get involved at the mall, why he left Mindy at the mercy of Alexis and Brittany, and me and Clay in the middle. I really expected more from Austin. His gold used to set him apart from all the other boys, and now it seemed like he wasn't any different.

I couldn't worry about him right now. I needed the quickest results I could find. I paged backwards in the book holding my violet to my lips, scanning the words on the pages. Nothing was right. I couldn't make sense of it.

I drank my glass of juice, put it in the sink, and walked into the parlor with the music book open on my forearms so that I could lay it right on the ledge where it belonged on the piano. I was going to stare at it while I played for as long as I felt like it. I hoped the music would clear my head of thoughts that were too rich to separate, either by color or feeling.

I couldn't have played for longer than a minute when pink stirred the air. I agitated the angry passion of that Slam Book by pounding out the music from the piano. I soaked the air with more pink, constructing the vision of the Slam Book from my head. I whisked through the pages of the music book to the pink ones, thin slices of the ruby red grapefruit I loved so, transparent coats of pink frosting that a little princess licked off her finger when she stole a smear from the cake. I tried to shred the awful feelings I knew all those girls planted in that Slam Book and replace them with these sugary pink ones so that I could stomach them to finish what I had started.

All I've ever been able to do up until now is read the colors and try to listen to them. But the music, the piano playing. It has been the connection. The song seemed to open up a pathway to Mom. Up until now, my knowledge of color was useless, powerless. Even wrong sometimes. I had to wonder what I'm supposed to do with my reading of the colors and listening to others by playing each of these songs. There's no one to tell me or show me. How am I supposed to figure it out with just Dad to try to explain it to me? He can't read the colors like I can or play the music like I can. Why did Mom leave this to me to figure out all by myself? I think I actually spoke that last question. I banged on the piano keys in frustration. I knew that wouldn't get me anywhere. I took a deep breath and tried to focus again.

I learned from the music that my mother used to play with me. Seated beside her, I would listen and watch her fingers spread over the keys as if she were skating on ice. Smooth but sharp movements dancing to the rhythms, telling a story that I could see and hear inside my heart. The colors pouring out in front of my eyes, the ones I didn't want to talk about because I thought I was the only one who could see them. She never told me that she could see them too.

When the house phone rang, which it rarely did anymore now that Dad and I used our own cellphones, my fingers stopped playing the song. The colors were silenced, and I was sitting looking at the pink page of the book seeing just the black notes written on the staffs in no particular order. It took me a moment to release my gaze and answer the phone.

Detective Monroe said he was glad I had answered the phone to give me the good news. They had summoned the phone records to show that that text messages had been sent to me, but the messages were too simple to prove any harassment charges based on them. Perfect. Exactly what I had thought. So what was the good news, I wondered, as the detective's words came out stunted and distracted.

They had the Slam Book. The pink one, he said. I know he wasn't imagining rare steak too pink and bloody to eat, like I was. I tried to picture bubble gum or cotton candy while he told me there was evidence that he couldn't share in detail. What he could tell me was that they had identified an individual who was blaming Ms. Stine for Mindy's murder although it was all a hoax, a lie. There was also mention of targeting me for the embarrassment of the fight in the cafeteria. I simmered inside, thanking the detective for his time. Justice served. Did he feel like Atticus Finch did when he figured out the crime?

I tried not to feel completely satisfied with the outcome, because that wasn't really the point, that I should feel some sense of accomplishment for all of this coming to an end. What was important was that Alexis wouldn't be able to bully anyone anymore. Not girls like me. Not teachers like Ms. Stine.

I was glad that Alexis wouldn't be back in my English class in January when school resumed. I could finish out the court scene with Austin and play out the ending that I wanted to see.

This gold paper was very much like the wrapping paper my mother used to wrap the flowers at the shop. It was hard to write with pen on the tissue-like inside, so she wrote on the gold side.

My Little Violet,
Making a good meal is part talent, part hard work, and part timing. The right combination of ingredients will serve a feast for many.

Chapter 19

THE next few days were long. Dad was at work, and Breck was helping his Dad with some other houses he was trying to get ready to put on the market after the New Year. Mindy used to have her mother pick me up on days like this, and we'd go to the mall to seek out the after-Christmas sales and meet up with other friends who weren't out of town visiting relatives for the break from school. But I didn't have anyone like that anymore.

I was moping around the kitchen. I had eaten breakfast already, and I wasn't hungry yet but looked in the refrigerator for something. I hadn't any idea what I expected was going to happen when I opened the door. The same leftovers sat there alongside the carton of milk and eggs, the only two fresh things in there. I closed the door and walked back over to the kitchen table where I had cleaned out my notebooks for my classes so that I'd be organized for the return to school in January.

I had finished reading the novel for English class, and I made a few more notes on our case for class that we'd hopefully have the chance to present when we got back to school. I was pretty confident that Ms. Stine would let us do that. I gathered up the papers, matched up their edges in a stack that I tapped against the table top, and I stuck it into my English notebook.

The doorbell rang. For a moment I felt like the first grader who read books and heard stern lectures about opening the door for strangers without asking first who was on the other side of the door. What would I do if it really happened to me? I never knew. Without realizing it at the time, the colors would have transformed the stranger into someone more familiar, someone I could read.

Walking through the hall to the parlor, I wanted to look first through the parlor window. Whoever it was most likely was coming to see me, and that was unsettling. There was little color to read. It was too faint to tell for sure.

Ms. Stine was standing at the door.

"Ms. Stine," I said pleasantly but unsure. "This is a surprise."

"I'm sure it is, Violet. How did you and your dad make it through the holiday?" she asked with polite concern.

"Okay, I guess." I knew that didn't really say much. "It passed, and there will be better." I said it with more conviction than I felt. And somehow, I thought that Ms. Stine could sense that. "And you?" I added politely.

"Well enough. But, it's time we had a talk, Violet." She was surrounded by a vague color that I could see though not entirely read, yet I felt I could trust her. Out of the neckline of her simple black dress, she pulled out a slim black cord, just like mine. Floating on the cord was a stone made of jade. It was oval in shape and had a greasy luster to it. The depth of the center was an intense emerald color with fine touches of violet shining through its edges.

She reached out and grasped my violet with a steady hand. Holding her jade at the same time, I was overcome with peace like I feel when I'm playing the piano. As if everything were balanced at once, she let go of my violet.

I nodded like a two-year-old not fully understanding what she meant. Like the words had lost their meaning but I knew by her tone that something was important.

"Let's go find your mother," she said matter-of-factly, as if my mother was at work instead of gone. She waited while I grabbed my jacket, and I made sure I had my phone. There was a journey

I seemed ready for without having fully understood how to start it. There was a link between her jade and my violet that had to be explained, and I was pretty sure that I was going to get more than just that answer today.

I sent Dad a text message after getting into Ms. Stine's car with her. As a familiar melody played low in the background, we headed to Hershey's Sweet Lights.

I took hold of my violet on our way, the twenty minute drive feeling so long. Ms. Stine filled it with the story though. The story of my secret. I thought I was the only one who could read the colors, but I couldn't have been more wrong. My mother could see the colors too. She just couldn't read them and listen to their truth as I was able to do.

My mother's color is rose, Ms. Stine said, like her name. Red with a little yellow in it so that it has an essence of pink, almost melon, she surmised. In order for me to live my life, she had to vanish from my life. Ms. Stine reminded me about my stay in the hospital.

I remembered how sick I felt, how tired, like I was dying.

"You could've died, Violet. We're never sure how compatible our gifts will be until we turn thirteen."

My Bat Mitzvah, I thought.

"Your mother realized that you were learning about all the nuances of your gift. You told her so after your Bat Mitzvah. She prepared to have to leave, but she waited to see if she was right, if you'd really start losing your life to let your gift live. Because your love for each other is so strong, a bond between mother and daughter, it becomes dangerous. The ability to read colors, the power, the gift, whatever you want to call it, becomes too strong when you're together."

So, I *was* responsible for sending Mom away. "Please tell me there was nothing I could've done to keep Mom close to me and Dad. I would do anything."

The music can help me listen to someone's thoughts, so maybe it has other power too. I let my memory sink back again to the music that my mother used to play with me. Listening and learning from her. Teaching me about reading the music on the page, learning the notes. Creamy colors would spout into the air from her masterpieces, so she could tell me a story that I could see and hear through the colors. I was not the only one who could see them. I told Ms. Stine that I found the book though, the music book. She nodded but didn't say another word, although I knew there was more to say.

I watched the familiar landmarks go by and the cars we passed as if in slow motion. It was agonizing. I was still holding my violet and looked at the leaves on the stem hugging the cord. The leaves were jade, just like Ms. Stine's. It was the jade leaves protecting me all the time, lying open and vulnerable while giving strength to the violet so that it could hold on to its life and glean vitality from the world's colors around me.

I sat and thought, trying to make sense of it all. "You can see the colors too, can't you?"

Ms. Stine nodded again and pressed her lips together trying to decide whether to smile or speak. She sighed. We pulled off the main road onto the path towards the entrance to the light display. As it was not yet dusk, there was nothing to see except dark outlines of wires and light bulbs, looking dead and spiritless. It was hard to see what shapes and scenes the creations were supposed to become without their illumination and their colors.

We remained on the path towards Hershey's Sweet Lights. The shadow of the car was barely hidden beyond thicker trees that guarded the edge. We started on another road that diverged from the path, only dirt and stone. Mounds of ice and snow bumped the car up and down as we maneuvered quite slowly, deeper into the woods where Hershey's Sweet Lights told its tale in lights. A small cabin, newer than I'd expect to find, revived the darkness from under the trees as it sat in a clearing. The light seemed to linger on its roof with a glow like a sunset, like a rosy halo of gold.

I felt my violet come to life on my chest. And, Ms. Stine glanced at me when I sharply sucked in my breath. She smiled then and stopped the car in front of the cabin.

Stepping into the main room of the small house, a wall with a large bay window let in light from my right. It was surprisingly well lit for a dark, rich wood that covered the room as if in chocolate. An average-sized desk in the center was made of cherry, I think, because it too was dark, rich, and had a heavy cushioned chair behind it that sat empty so that I could see the upholstery pins wrinkling the fabric on the cushion. It was high-backed like the chair Dad sits in to watch me play the piano and listen to the music. Her music. Opposite the window was a wall that intrigued me the most. The violet caught my eye first, the purple flower pressed underneath a slab of smooth, clear glass reflecting the clouds from the blue sky across the room.

On the desk sat a picture that I recognized except that it wasn't my mother sitting on the bed looking beyond the camera lens. Ms. Stine posed in a similar spot on the bed that now rested in my bedroom with my quilt to cover it and my tears poured into its pillows. I hadn't noticed the similarities before. The coffee brown hair. The telling eyes that met mine with kindness, love even.

"Your mother is my sister, Violet."

The house was not much more than this large room, but I had to wonder if my mother was here. Ms. Stine had to sense my longing. She hugged me close then, and I felt her turmoil churning through the jade around her neck. There was more.

"Your mother saw that you had to begin to control other people's energies; otherwise, they were strangling you, suffocating you."

"Killing me, you mean. She was afraid that they were killing me." It was true. That was how I felt sometimes.

"And she couldn't stand to see it happen to her daughter. She left because she loved you. If she stayed, you couldn't have fully used your gift."

"But she was being selfish. Leaving us...," frustrated tears pooled in my violet eyes.

"I suppose, yes. But, she believed in you, that you'd be able to find quality in life. And, you did it. You found the book of colors, you have Grandma's piano, and you read the colors. You can hear what others are thinking. You are learning to control and understand them." Ms. Stine said it with pride in her voice, but she was consoling herself as well as me. No doubt she missed my mother too.

"What do I do with the book? Can't she come back to us? Where is she?" I asked these questions thinking that maybe I had control of bringing my mother back to me and my father. I felt lucky to have my great-grandmother's piano, not even knowing that playing music was part of my gift.

"I can't answer that for sure, Violet. The older you get, the more your gift will change and grow with you. That's why your mom waited; because she thought that maybe her own ability to read colors might change enough to allow you two to be together. Like I said, your love was so strong..." She was shaking her head just barely, but I saw it. I felt her doubt. She shrugged her shoulders and crossed her arms.

"So, that's why I could never see your colors like I could for most everyone else. Because you're like me. Like us. " I was beginning to understand. Not accept it but understand for now. This time I nodded my head. I noted her necklace. "You must be Jade. Jade Stine?"

"Yes, Violet. Aunt Jade. And, I will help you. I promise. I'm just not entirely sure what we can do."

"That's all Mom ever asked of me...." I looked around the cabin then, hoping to see a glimpse of the rosy image I had seen that night at Friendly's after the field hockey game. I didn't see it, but I knew she was there. "And, now that I know she can see me, that has made all the difference."

We stayed for a little while longer in the cabin. Ms. Stine, or Aunt Jade, explained to me that this was a caretaker's cabin for some of the gardens surrounding the town of Hershey. And my grandmother, as well as her mother, were caretakers to the gardens, tending to varieties of flowers that would be cut for arrangements in the home and offices of Milton Hershey, the founder of the town. And the founder of the chocolate, among other things. The present gardens are expansive, intricate designs that visitors long to learn from, stroll in, and declare their love in. Children watch butterflies burst in bunches of colors, and lovers can hold hands by the trickle of the fountains and dream. This was the place where my mother and her sister learned to grow plants and flowers while they practiced but hid the true talents they shared.

Aunt Jade didn't know whether it was the magic of the forest, the sweetness of the town, or the genes in their blood, or the right combination of them all, but somehow the women of our family saw the colors. The gift had the potential to heal the past and change the future, but learning its power took its toll and the mother-daughter bond had to give way. It happened to my grandmother and my mother. This was the reason that Aunt Jade didn't marry and have a child, she admitted. It was too painful to watch my mother have to let go of me. Because, all she knew before that was that her mother had taken the very same path. She had to let go of them.

My father was told about the pattern, but he loved my mother so much, he was willing to take the risk despite the possibility of shortening their time together. It made me love him so much more. He was the one who had sacrificed too without any control over any of the outcomes. I wasn't sure how he'd take my new understanding of it all, but I didn't want to let him down. I remembered the night he told me about some of what he knew, but this was far more. I knew it was important to him that he still had me as a part of Mom with him.

My brain was overwhelmed with all of this new information, but it actually made me feel better to understand. When Aunt Jade coupled her jade with my violet, there was a balance; I was protected, and a doorway had opened for me with new colors, bright and vivid, that could bring me and my father happiness in the future. Did I think that I could break the secret and find a way for Mom to be with us, to be close to me? Couldn't we even just call each other on the phone? I couldn't help but to think about it.

We left the little cabin in the woods, agreeing to come back someday. Aunt Jade said she comes here for solace, for time away from the real world, so to speak. I didn't see a piano there, so I didn't think that I could play music there to try to communicate with Mom. But I would like to get to know Aunt Jade better, and know my mother better. Maybe this was the place to do that.

We headed home then. I was exhausted with the emotional upheaval of the day, especially now that I had more to understand about myself and my history than I had ever expected before. I wanted to share this with Dad, but I was afraid it would tear his heart open again. I wanted him to feel something other than blue.

When Aunt Jade dropped me off, and I thanked her with a hug, I felt a new closeness that I had missed in my mother for over a year now. If I couldn't have my mother back in my life, I knew that Aunt Jade was charged with my safety and knew my secret. I finally had someone to turn to when I had questions about my gift. I still resented being made me so special and different because it made me so sad and lonely sometimes, but maybe I could do something about it. I invited her inside and asked her if she'd stay for dinner now that she had shared the secret, but she said she should go.

After she left, I wondered why she didn't stay. I was confused by the reason she couldn't share the connection out in the open with everyone. Despite the secret, there must be a problem or a danger in our having a relationship. Maybe if she and I became too close, the same danger would erupt. I always felt like I knew a lot of things that other people didn't because of my gift, yet this secret left me not knowing.

Back and forth my feelings jumped, frustrating me while exciting me. I didn't have any answers. I still had a problem. Dad would be arriving home soon, so I had decided to make dinner. There was nothing edible in the refrigerator; this was not going to take my mind off my problem. I laughed out loud to myself. That wouldn't work. I'd think about dinner later and the colors now.

I opened the refrigerator, poured myself a drink of the Italian mineral water, and took a sip, letting the bubbles fizz on my tongue and help me relax and think more clearly. I took the colors book, or the music book, or whatever it truly was, and carried it and my glass of sparkling water up to my bedroom. Maybe I'd straighten up the house and wash a load of laundry. I didn't know what to do with myself. I couldn't wait till Dad got home so that I'd at least be able to share what I learned today with him about my past and about the possibility of bringing Mom back. I wished Aunt Jade would stay and open up this bond we have. I think it would help us both.

I sat down on my bed and set my glass on my nightstand. I turned to look at Mom's picture and wondered still what she was looking at or thinking. Maybe she was missing her mother just as I was missing mine.

I closed my eyes then and knew that with Mom's leaving, she was just trying to purge the pain. So that I felt none and she felt none, yet we were still in longing without each other. I opened my eyes. The silver box was sitting in my closet this whole time. I picked myself up to go over to it and open it up. I untied the ribbon, gold-trimmed from the flower shop, just like the one around the flowers

I found with the book. I took out each of the messages Mom wrote to me and smoothed them out carefully. All those notes Mom left for me in the flower shop in case something happened here at home and I couldn't get her back. I couldn't leave them there. Just realizing her renewed presence in my life has helped me be stronger already. I understood I had it inside me—whether I was reading the colors or not, listening to thoughts or not.

All of the paper. Many of Mom's notes were written on the same paper as the pages in the book. I had them all along. Lessons about life. Songs that told me what to do and guided me as Mom would have. This music wasn't just for my ears. I was supposed to share it. And I knew just who needed to listen the most.

Chapter 20

THE color violet is more than just my name. It is the color by which we readers can identify each other. It is the clearest color of the spirit. To most everyone else, violet symbolizes royalty because of the expensive ink that kings and queens could afford to dye their royal clothes. I am no queen. I am sure that I am not destined to royalty nor did I have such respectable beginnings. I can see colors, just like my mother could, and her mother before her, and I suppose it passed on.

But I can read the colors, too, by looking and listening. And, I've learned to use what I know. I don't use them to find out the questions on a test or to see who will be voted Homecoming Queen. I've used them to save people from themselves and each other. That might not sound that exciting, but for now, that's all I know how to do. I'm still only 14, and Aunt Jade says that I have a lot of growing up to do despite the losses I've already endured and the battles I've already fought. She also said that it's okay if I use my gift for personal reasons. I can use it to help people. I try to use it to help my Dad pretty often. I help Mindy's parents and her little brother almost every day right now. I help them get through each day now. I hope they'll need me less as time goes by. That would make me feel useful. I feel so much more important than I ever have in my life.

I know there will always be someone in the way. People like

Alexis or Brittany. As I become more skilled at listening and understanding the colors I read, and at playing the piano, I can do better things in this world. And, then I hope maybe I can change the people who are the hardest to reach.

I've mastered playing the Pink Panther theme in honor of Clay. He makes me laugh. He was always close by and protected me, and I always felt like I could trust his colors. I feel lucky about that. I've got my own special bodyguard. Inspector Clay.

We returned after the Winter Break subdued; just trying to remember what day it was so that we knew which classes we had was task enough. I knew I had chorus during activity period this morning, so that was a good start. I was actually considering finding the band director and asking him if he'd still be interested in my joining the band. I think I am ready to play the piano in front of an audience now. They won't know whether I'm listening to their thoughts or the music as long as my tune is in key. Honestly, I just want to help our school get back to the way it was, the way it felt before we lost Mindy. Before Winter Solstice became a horror story to tell before Christmas instead of Halloween.

I have been practicing at home a lot, especially on Wednesday nights when Dad isn't home and neither is Mindy. Breck comes over. After he fixed the treadmill on one of his first visits, he began to trek around the house while I play, and he searches for something to fix for my Dad, just to help out. Sometimes he'll make a batch of chocolate chip cookies. He doesn't usually just sit and listen to me play. But I know he's listening from wherever he is. He's good company. He's not my mother, of course, but he is becoming a companion worthy of the violet color of his. It's funny how that color keeps making an appearance.

We finally completed our court case in English class. At the beginning of the project I was scared to speak out for others, a person I may not have identified with or fully understood, but someone I knew who deserved respect for being an individual, even if he was different for some reason. Different like I am. Knowing that there is very likely an enemy sowing the opposite ideas, ready to avenge and stand up against what I stood for fed my fears. And I was right to be scared. What I hadn't anticipated was being attacked by someone like me, someone who just didn't know any better. It made me want to share what I learned to try to help make a better world one little mind at a time. I still knew that a tiny bit of courage inside my heart that I had never tended before was sprouting finally; I could wear my violet proudly instead of using it as a crutch to save myself.

Ms. Stine reminded us that we couldn't rewrite a classic, just learn from it. I didn't work quite the same with Austin as we had before losing Mindy. I guessed Mindy would still be jealous, even just a little. If she were still here, I'd play her a song that would match her melon color so that she could fall head over heels for someone without the gold that I misunderstood in Austin. He taught me a lesson too. I shouldn't always trust the colors I can read without questioning them. But, he is still has goodness inside; he just may not be as perfect as Mindy thought he was.

I took the evaluation form that Ms. Stine had given us with our grade and comments on the trial, stuck it inside my notebook with the copy of my novel, and left class uplifted. I was still walking with my shoulders a little higher than normal and smiling with a sense of purpose. I wondered if lawyers who know they have survived their first battle feel the same way.

I sit with Clay at lunch most every day now.

"How was English today?" he usually asks. I try to keep my violet charm a crystal clear purple during English class so that I can read the colors clearly. I don't grapple anymore with wanting to listen to Alexis' thoughts through her colors and guess her intentions. She is a master chameleon, after all. It was too bad she'd never read all those notes Mom had left for me. Even though I still struggle with Mom being gone, I want to read the colors, so I hum a song from the book sometimes, to preserve the peace in English class and remind me that I am strong.

"Killing her with kindness," I answer. It's like a cloak I wear on the outside, keeping my secrets underneath.

I felt bad that I couldn't help Brittany the way I had planned to help Alexis from being such a bully. It had been Brittany who had been shouting at Mindy at the mall more than Alexis—name-calling before we arrived at school for Winter Solstice. And, it had been Alexis who had put her up to stabbing Mindy and killing her. As I had correctly deciphered at the very time of the investigation by the police, Brittany had only been able to confront us because she had Alexis by her side. She never would've done anything like that alone. Yet, Alexis would walk away free to continue to execute her free will on anyone in her path while Brittany, unfortunately, would be serving a sentence in a youth detention facility. I don't blame her entirely. She killed my friend, and I hope she remembers that for the rest of her life. But I hope that someone teaches her to stand up for herself, to recognize gifts that she may have so that she doesn't find herself victimized by a bully like Alexis ever again. Brittany was a victim too. I feel sorry for her, yet I forgive her because of that.

Cropsie, or Mr. Christopher, still keeps to himself. He likes life like that. I don't blame him. But I check on him. It must be hard to be by yourself all the time. Breck and I try to go over there regularly. I think he likes it, although he'd never say so. He still never says much at all.

After school that first day back, Dad and Breck picked me up, and we drove straight to the retirement home to visit Poppop. With everything that had happened to Mindy, we had never made it over there for the holiday. We brought him a few new pairs of pants and shirts and a box of chocolate. I hoped we'd still be able to sing some songs together even though Christmas was over. I liked to sing with him. And, I know the music made him feel better too. Listening to him sing with me does him well, almost like that box of chocolates does.

I had left a welcome basket at our new neighbors' house just as I said I would. Aunt Jade had given me some ideas of what they might like. I placed some fruit and flowers in the basket and added some handmade babysitting coupons so that they might call on me. If I couldn't have a sibling of my own, I was happy to take care of their little girl for the time being. And maybe I could teach her to play the piano or sing a song. Or even just the colors. I thought she'd like that.

Aunt Jade was starting to come around a little more often. She still kept to herself a lot, spending time at the cabin, especially when days like Mother's Day arrived. Now that I was going to the high school next year, it didn't much matter if I called her Aunt Jade. And I wanted to. She was getting used to it. Being loved, that is.

I've learned a lot about myself in these short few months of eighth grade. A lot of what I learned was straight from Ms. Stine's English class, in fact.

It's okay if I don't condemn the guilty. That's not my job. I'm not the judge. It's hard enough to worry about my own mistakes. And the ones that I've witnessed. Maybe someday I could take on that queen of a task, but for now, I will settle for fulfilling the gift I was given and hoping it makes a difference.

On our way to visiting Poppop, my phone chimed with a text. I showed it to Breck. He barely smiled and continued his conversation with Dad in the front seat. I typed a message, leaned back in my seat and pressed send. Looking out the window, the violet twinkled a little brighter in my eyes. And I was pretty sure that Mom could tell.

CPSIA information can be obtained at www.ICGtesting.com
Printed in the USA
LVOW040931010412

275633LV00001B/18/P